THAT'S
NOT
MY
STYLE

THAT'S
NOT
MY
STYLE

by Mary Anderson

Atheneum 1984 New York

Library of Congress Cataloging in Publication Data

Anderson, Mary
   That's not my style.

   SUMMARY: John alienates his parents by refusing to go into the family butcher business and instead spends his time eavesdropping on neighbors gathering material for an epic novel.
   [1. Parent and child—Fiction.   2. Authorship—Fiction] I. Title.
PZ7.A5444Th 1983   [Fic]   82-13772
ISBN 0-689-30968-6

Copyright © 1983 by Mary Anderson
All rights reserved
Published simultaneously in Canada by McClelland and Stewart Ltd
Composition by American–Stratford Graphic Services, Inc.,
Brattleboro, Vermont
Manufactured by Fairfield Graphics, Fairfield, Pennsylvania
Designed by Marjorie Zaum
First printing January 1983
Second printing December 1983
Third printing July 1984

To Davey . . .

THAT'S
NOT
MY
STYLE

Chapter 1

— — — — — — — — — — — — —

I was sitting in the bathroom (the only private place with a lock) wondering why parents insist on insinuating themselves into a guy's life.

What's it their business?

Isn't it enough they brought me into the world, fed me, put a roof over my head? Do they have to know what I'm *doing* all the time?

Look, I'm not ungrateful. I know my folks invested lots of time in the first sixteen years of my life. And I'm truly thankful Mom didn't push my baby carriage into traffic or anything; or that Dad didn't beat me with a pig whip. But now the job's done. Shouldn't I be allowed to handle the rest of the deal myself?

As far as I'm concerned, my course is charted, my

fate sealed. There's no turning back, no room for discussion. I'm going to be a writer. Period! Their simple acceptance of this simple fact would make life exceedingly simple.

So who said life should be easy, right? Believe me, I know. Being a creative person can be the pits. And hazardous to your health. Most of the time, everyone thinks you're out of your bird. Hence, the necessity to seek refuge in the bathroom.

At that moment, Mom was pounding on the door, eager to discuss the events of the morning. Ignoring her incessant banging, I continued to record the day's journalistic observations. But I had a graphic vision of a female fist thrusting its way through the painted glass panel any moment.

"You can't hide in there all day, Janos!"

Mom knows I hate being called that. It reminds me of some character from an old Boris Karloff movie, one who invents the death ray or something. Thank goodness my birth certificate says John. But Mom hangs onto old ways, often reverting to Hungarian, even though she and Dad have been here since they were kids. Both their families fled Hungary during the revolution of the fifties. Unfortunately, they brought with them lots of crazy Old World customs, like believing in the Evil Eye and the importance of family ties, which actually translates into butting their nose into a guy's business.

"Mr. Mancusso won't stand for it any more, Janos."
(She'd started shouting and I knew Hungarian epithets

might soon be forthcoming.) "If he finds you snooping outside his door once more, he's calling the cops."

"It's not snooping," I shouted back, hurriedly finishing off my notes. "It's *research*."

"Whatever you call it, the police are gonna hear about it."

Well, maybe I did go too far this time. Being apprehended at a person's door with a glass stuck to one's ear could be considered incriminating evidence in some circles. But I couldn't help it. Mancusso and his wife are classic examples of a contemporary couple in the throes of every social problem modern society can dish out. When they start arguing, their conversations take on dramatic proportions only the theater of the absurd could encompass! Unfortunately, the front door of their apartment's so thick, I can't always hear everything. So naturally, I was forced to resort to the old glass-at-the-ear. (Which works damn well, by the way.)

Why does Mancusso persist in thinking my objective journalistic research is snooping? As I see it, I was hanging around, minding my own business. Okay, maybe it's Mancusso's business, too, but that's my point.

Every true aspiring writer must soak up the atmosphere around him. How else can human relationships be accurately recorded?

So maybe I am a snoop . . . a nosey-parker . . . a busybody. Or, to be more literary (which I always try to be) . . . a voyeur.

Want the dictionary definition? It's one of the many

at my fingertips. No, never mind. *Webster's* calls me a pervert. Of course, that has to do with sex; and that's not my interest as far as the Mancussos are concerned. Not exclusively, anyway. Their knockdown, drag-out fights are what fascinate me. How could a fervent observer of society not be attracted?

"Janos, your father'll be home for lunch soon. He'll want to use the bathroom."

From the tone of Mom's voice, I knew she was calming down. She'd probably realized she could postpone the topic until lunchtime, letting Dad deal with the latest humiliation I'd heaped upon their heads.

"If you want to sulk, you've got a perfectly good room to do it in."

Sulk. How juvenile! Would the great Hemingway sulk if he were thwarted from creating a full-bodied characterization? Indeed not. He'd push on, against all odds.

Ernest Hemingway's book of letters is my Bible, which I keep by my bedside at all times. He has advice for every situation, including this one. Know what Papa said? (His friends and relatives always called him Papa. Since I consider myself his spiritual son, I don't think he'd mind my doing so, too.) He said, "For God's sake, write and write truly, no matter who or what it hurts. . . . That's what dries a writer up, not listening. That is where it all comes from. Seeing. Listening."

"Did you hear me, Janos? Get the hell out of there!"

With E. H.'s words as inspiration, I closed my notebook. Despite parental pestering, I'd managed to remember most of Mancusso's pithy comments, intact.

With renewed dedication, I opened the bathroom door.

Mom stood menacingly on the other side, her arms folded across her chest, a wooden spoon clamped in her right hand, and the sternest expression she could muster wrinkling up her reddish-brown eyebrows. She tried maintaining a look of authority, but one vagrant curl slipped down her forehead into her eyes, and she was forced to blow it away; thus destroying the illusion. She couldn't have pulled it off, anyway. I'm at least a foot taller, so she's got to lean over and look up at me in order to yell effectively.

"It's not enough your room is piled high with books and junk. Now you're moving into the bathroom. Find some place else for your papers and pencils. There are certain bodily needs that can't be tended to elsewhere."

"Really," I said with practiced superiority. "And which particular room might I enter to tend the needs of my soul?"

Mom tossed me a disdainful glance. "Maybe someday you'll prove to be the genius you seem to think you are. Maybe even make it into college. But right now, your grades stink to high heaven! And also right now, your father and I still have more education than you do. Four years of high school each, Janci. That makes eight years altogether. So don't give me any literary attitude."

I tucked my notebook under my arm and proceeded toward my bedroom.

"Where are you going? Get back in that bathroom and wash for lunch."

"You just made me get *out*."

"Whatever you do in there, it's not cleaning. The soap's always dry. Go back and wash your hands."

It's hard to imagine the ridiculous depths some mothers can sink to. What perverse instinct would make her examine the *soap*?

Retracing my steps, I slammed the bathroom door, turned on the faucets full blast, hurled the soap into the sink, until bubbles and wet spray spit out like a fountain. That ought to make her happy!

As I washed up, I tried holding onto E. H.'s words of wisdom. But I couldn't help thinking he'd never met Mom!

Weekend lunches are a ritual in our house. Mom and Dad love to sit around the table, extolling the virtues of togetherness and grumbling about their imbecilic offspring. During the week, Mom works in Dad's butcher shop, just blocks from our apartment. I suppose the bank owns most of it, but it's their pride and joy. Dad worked and saved for years, hacking his way through other people's meat until he could afford a place of his own.

Though hard to comprehend, Dad actually *enjoys* being a butcher; descended from a long line of them, at that. There's a certain morbid dedication in the way he fillets a steak or debones a chicken breast. He gets an almost religious tone in his voice when he proclaims: "I'm going to the store." . . . like he was going to church or something.

I was ten when the shop first opened. Dad and Mom coyly announced they had a surprise for me. (I thought it was a new bike.) Instead, they proudly took me by the hand and led me up to Broadway. They unlocked the door of the new store, and eyes gleaming with joy, Dad gave me a tour of the brand new butcher blocks and hooks.

Leading me into the fully-stocked freezer room, he gestured toward the sides of beef, pig's carcasses and smoked hams. A lump caught in his throat as he informed me, "All this is ours now, Janos."

At the time, I was too young and too disappointed about the bike to note the humor in the situation. Dad envisioned himself as an aristocratic landowner, surveying his plantation: the noble heritage he'd one day pass on to his only son.

All I could think of was the story he'd once told me when I was little. In the sixteenth century, a Hungarian nobleman led the peasants in a country-wide revolt. For his efforts, he was roasted alive in the marketplace. I guess "Our People" have had a penchant for roasted flesh ever since.

Anyway, I was appalled and became a vegetarian on the spot. No, I'm exaggerating. But I can't bring myself to eat sections of animals that make it graphically clear which area they've been crudely hacked from. I'm okay with stew or even a hot dog, but a leg of lamb, a pig's foot or an oxtail makes my stomach roll over. And the sight of *tongue* can do me in altogether. Unfortunately, Dad's shop specializes in the good old European cuts of meat assiduously avoided in the supermarket. On any given day, oozing pig's heads, gnarled limbs, brains and innards can be viewed hanging limply in the window. Cannibal City, for all the world to see.

I know my attitude depresses Dad, so I avoid his butcher shop like the plague. But my distaste for his business hasn't prevented it from doing well. Dad's got quite a reputation in the neighborhood.

A word about the neighborhood. It's one of those upwardly mobile ones on the west side of Manhattan: sturdy old buildings, dating back to the turn of the century. Lots of them became rundown during the fifties. Following a mass exodus to the suburbs, they were turned into SRO's (single room occupancy). That's when the city began filling them up with mental out-patients: poor souls who walked around Broadway with one shoe, talking into milk cartons. Classic cases, every one. When I was little, my particular favorite was the Onion Bag Man, thus named because of the orange onion netting he wears over his head. He'd stand on Broadway by the subway entrance and mumble, "Nickel, please," from dawn to dusk. Unlike the postman, neither rain nor snow nor gloom of night kept him from his appointed task.

Then the brownstone craze hit the city. People began buying up every rundown building in sight. The larger ones were gutted and turned into co-ops. That's when the neighborhood took on its fascinating rich-poor mix. Many people, like my parents, who'd stayed on in their rent-controlled apartments, now shared the streets with the "Beautiful People," who'd returned from the suburbs or migrated from the East Side. Tired of over-priced ticky-tacky walls, they wanted high ceilings and a view of the Hudson River. Artists, actors, lawyers, they all came back.

Of course, the Onion Bag Man never left. But now he's changed his pitch to "Quarter, please." Inflation strikes us all!

All these folk (with the possible exception of Mr. Onion Bag) frequent Dad's butcher shop. The wealthy come for filet mignon, veal steaks and prosciutto; the poor for liver and pig's feet. Mom and Dad stand behind the counter, dispensing their largesse equally among them all.

As they're so fond of saying: "Only in America."

"Are your hands clean?" asked Mom, peppering the goulash with paprika for the third time.

I nodded and sat down at the kitchen table.

As the clock donged the half-hour, Dad came through the door, shouted, "Hello, Anna," then proceeded into the bathroom. He returned in a moment and asked, "Have we got a leak in there or something? The walls are soaking wet."

Mom flashed me a look. "I'll check on it after lunch. Busy morning, Joszef?"

"Pretty good. There was a run on kielbasa. That TV chef must've been making some sausage dish on his show last night. Whatever he makes Friday, we get a run on, Saturday."

"What was it last week?" she asked. "Venison?"

"In duck sauce." Dad nodded.

I poked at my stew. Massacring deer wasn't bad enough, they had to squeeze the juice from ducks, too!

Dad wiped his moustache with a napkin. "Know what Mrs. Weizer said to me this morning? 'Mr. Sandor,' she said, 'it's a pleasure to walk in your store. Even the sawdust smells good.' Well, I told her, there's no reason for a butcher shop to smell like a slaughterhouse."

I pushed my plate away.

"Aren't you hungry?" asked Dad.

"Not very."

I'd never fully confided my meat aversion to my folks. It would be like denying my religion or something. (Maybe I'd run out and grab some pizza later.)

"Janci's got no appetite because he's waiting for you to talk to him," Mom explained.

"What now?" asked Dad suspiciously.

"Mr. Mancusso. He caught Janos listening at his door again. He says he's a pervert."

"What's the matter with you, boy? Are you nuts or what? What do you keep bothering those people for?"

It's nothing personal," I insisted. "Just clinical investigation."

"When someone keeps staring at you in the hallway, you take it personal."

"Not in the hallway this time," Mom explained. "Right at their front door. With a glass to his ear!"

"You *are* crazy," shouted Dad. "Do you want to ruin my business? The Mancussos were good customers until you started spying on them. Now they'd rather walk to Brooklyn for a chicken, than set foot in my store. Is this what we've worked for all these years?"

"But is *is* nothing personal, Dad. Just think of me as a doctor, dissecting the ills of society."

"Now it's a doctor? I thought you wanted to be a writer."

"A *great* writer," I corrected.

"Excuse me. So tell me something. Where's all this potential I never see? You don't show it in school. Your English teacher's been giving you C's."

"That's because Mr. Holloway's an idiot! Know what this week's assignment is? 'My Life as a Pencil.'"

Mom blinked. "Maybe he wants to beef up your imagination. There must be some reason for it."

"Only to Holloway," I argued. *"He's* the woodenhead . . . the only one whose geneological tree can be directly traced back to a maple."

Mom giggled, until Dad darted her a look of disgust and she stifled it.

"Swell, Anna," he said, tearing into the Italian bread. "Encourage him. He's not crazy enough?"

"I can't help it, Joszef; he puts things so colorfully. I don't know why he doesn't get A's."

"Because instead of writing, he's got his ear stuck to people's doors. Don't tell me you believe all his doctor baloney. If he'd just knuckle down and . . ."

As our typical Saturday luncheon continued, I found myself wishing I'd hidden my notebook under the table. I bet my folks had no idea how many times they referred to *meat* in their everyday conversation: beef, baloney, knuckles. Fascinating.

The remainder of the argument would be exclusively about yours truly, so I decided not to listen. I was intrigued by a far more interesting picture I'd just created: dumb old Holloway, wandering aimlessly through a forest decimated by fire, frantically calling out the names of his relatives, trying in vain to recognize one stump from the other. Here was pathos, human interest. Maybe I'd write that idiotic essay, after all. All it needed was a change of title. I'd call it *"Your* Life as a Pencil," dedicate it to Holloway and trace his family history directly back to Pinocchio. It would get me another C, but it would be good for a laugh.

That's all my English class is good for, anyway: laughs. Holloway wouldn't know a great writer if he bumped into Shakespeare in an otherwise deserted alley. Once, I had the temerity to attempt discussing Hemingway's *The Sun Also Rises* with him. "Ah yes," he said pompously, "the lost generation. Mindless, shiftless, pointless individuals. I can see why they appeal to you, John." That put a damper on any further literary conversations we might've had. Besides, I suspect his reading preferences run toward porno-fantasies.

Me, I'm a Hemingway man; but Faulkner's not bad, either. He did a damn good job of chronicling the life of the local Southern yokels he lived with. But E. H. was the man who cleaned up the language and jettisoned all the junk: don't use two words if one'll do . . . eliminate all the hogwash . . . can the baloney.

Now *I* was doing it! That ironic thought brought me back to reality and the conversation at hand.

"Hear me, Janos?" Dad shouted. "I want that promise from you now. Keep the hell away from Mancusso's door."

I considered the suggestion. Mr. and Mrs. Mancusso's fights had a definite pattern. Once they'd had a real wingding, they gave each other the silent treatment for days. That meant I wouldn't be missing out on any juicy slice-of-life conversations for a while. When they had at each other again, I could always try listening from the roof. The Mancussos are on the top floor, so the sound probably travels pretty well.

"Okay Dad, I promise."

"Good, now finish your lunch. That's prime beef in that goulash."

Chapter 2

_ _ _ _ _ _ _ _ _ _ _ _

. . . writing classics, I've always heard, takes some time
_. . . E.H._

Confidentially, the Mancussos are merely a minor
wheel in the great machinery of my master plan. Hemingway depicted the decadence of post-war Europe, Faulkner did the same for Mississippi. And I'll do it for New
York, my tiny part of it, anyway.

My neighbors are only a start. I've already begun
taking notes on some of the locals who hang around
Broadway: the pushers, hookers and street crazies, in the
fortune-telling parlors and bookie joints. But that's not
half of it. There are lots of rich, trendy couples poking
around in those fancy cheese stores.

I'm telling you, it's a microcosm. A person could live an entire life in a square mile radius and never run out of material. I plan for at least one chapter to take place in the Salvation Army Thrift Store. The varied types who pop in there could actually fill a book.

So I'm sure you see my poking around doorways and incurring the wrath of my folks is necessary for the success of my master plan.

Once Dad went back to work, I sequestered myself in my room. I lay on my bed, seeking solace from the shelves, piles, heaps and masses of books surrounding me. A plethora of books. A massive structure of paper and bindings growing out from the walls and stacked at least five feet high. To me, an edifice more noble than any cathedral. To Mom, a housekeeping problem she succinctly refers to as "Roach City."

On the rare occasion she's got guts enough to enter, she arms herself with a feather duster and a strong pair of stomping shoes.

"Cockroaches love the glue in these books. I hope you know you're feeding an army in here. They better not start backing up into my kitchen!"

Such comments always remind me of Don Marquis's *Archy and Mehitabel.* Archy: the indomitable little cockroach, who at night poured out his soul onto a newspaper office's typewriter. Archy: an incurable romantic, trying to deal with art *and* reality. Archy: a kindred spirit. How could I allow Mom to snuff out the life of any one insect, when I might be harboring a poet in the crowd!

It's also a protective mechanism. In light of the distinct vermin problem, Mom usually steers clear of my room altogether. That leaves me free to add to my book collection.

My books come from everywhere: the aforementioned Salvation Army, other second-hand stores, the street, the garbage and, of course, the library. My stack of overdues fills half a wall. I probably owe the city a million bucks, but I have three library cards in different names, so they haven't caught up with me yet.

My portable typewriter comes from La Salvation, too. Murphy, the guy who runs the place, let me have it for ten bucks.

Thinking of Murphy, I decided to jot down some further notes about the Salvation Army store. In my book, I plan to use it to illustrate modern socio-economics. A few years ago, there used to be great stuff in there for a quarter. Piles of clothes were thrown in bins like trash, and people had a great old time poking through it to find bargains. Then they painted the place, put everything on hangers and stuck tags on things. Prices skyrocketed and they lost all their business.

Then Murphy took over. He ignores the price tags. Whatever it is, it's yours for almost nothing if he likes your face. Eye contact and a kind word are priceless commodities to good old Murph.

Of course, it helps if you look like a bum, which isn't

hard for me. With so many books stacked in my room, I can never find any clothes. I wear the same thing every day, until Mom burns it. She insists I have half a dozen pairs of clean jeans and tee shirts folded away in a drawer somewhere. I've never bothered to look for them, and frankly, I think Mom's afraid to stick her hand in the drawer herself . . . one of Archy's cousins might attack. So, my condemned clothes stand me in good stead with Murph and keep the books coming my way for a nickel each.

I wish I could write an essay on Murphy, instead of that asinine treatise on a pencil. It really boils me to have my English class be a total waste of time. Especially when Holloway thinks he's doing us a favor . . . giving us the benefit of his knowledge . . . casting his pitiful pearls before swine.

This particular assignment was prefaced by his pretentious comment, "It will help you come to grips with fantasy." Damn, even his phraseology was loused up. One comes to grips with reality, jackass!

I was getting so churned up, I decided to actually write the damned essay. I went to my typewriter and pounded out the mythical story of Holloway's life; from tree stump, to puppet, to artificial, wooden, uninspired, deadheaded teacher in the public school system. It ran three pages, which I finished off with a pithy quote from Emerson: "If you would learn to write, it is in the street you must learn it. . . . The people and not the college is the writer's home."

That ought to let him know what I thought of his journey into fantasy!

This done, I settled down to the serious business of literature. I'd already given up any hope of sharpening my craft in school, and accepted the fact that any knowledge coming my way would be self-taught. I'd selected Ernest Hemingway as my teacher. I'd begun typing up his first novel, *The Sun Also Rises,* page by page, in my spare time. A guy learns a lot from reading, but actually typing out someone else's work is even better. It gets me into the bones of the writer, helps me analyze his construction.

Hemingway's first book is one of his minor works, but not without its good points. The dialogue is natural, he shoots straight from the hip and doesn't confuse the issue with unnecessary descriptions. No life-as-a-pencil garbage for E.H., thank you.

The book is about this guy who has his sex organs shot off or shot up during World War I. He and his friends go bumming around Paris and Spain, watching bull fights and getting blind drunk all the time. Meanwhile, he's in love with this English woman, but can't do much about it, if you know what I mean. Weak by today's standards, but pretty strong stuff at the time.

I typed out two chapters, to get my creative juices flowing. (That sappy assignment hadn't served the purpose.) I stuck them in my E.H. file, then typed out the notes on the Mancussos I'd made that morning. These went in a separate file, with all my other notes on the neighborhood. It was finally filling out, but I still hadn't figured how to assemble everything. My research was based on fact, but I knew, or assumed, at least, that the various accounts in my masterwork would have to be held together by fictional elements. (Whatever form it took, it would certainly be a masterwork. I'd settle for nothing less!)

It could turn into a total work of fiction or perhaps a combination of fact and fiction, as Truman Capote had done in *In Cold Blood*. Or maybe it would be best to tell it strictly like it is: rip the lid off the seething, tempestuous lives of the kooks, creeps, CPA's and closet Republicans intermingling on Broadway. Too much like soap opera? Maybe.

Hell, whatever it turned out to be, there was definitely enough background material for *more* than one book. Perhaps I'd write a trilogy or a quartet of books, each focusing on one ultra-colorful character. But as yet, I hadn't been as fortunate as Capote. Unlike him, my research hadn't put me in contact with a murderer who would ultimately wind up dangling from a rope. So far, the Mancussos' arguments were my only contact with violence. But there was time. I'd keep collecting background material until a character worthy of starring in my magnum opus appeared on the scene, either in my imagination or in reality. Yeah, some unknown character who'd pull the diverse elements together.

At the moment, the basic theme wasn't important. Getting down my impression of things while they were still sharp and relevant was my major concern. Besides, every writer is different, with his own distinct style. Vladimir Nabokov took tons of notes before writing anything. By the time he sat at the typewriter, he'd forgotten what all the notes were about. But he wrote great books. For the moment, I was content to consider my efforts a "work in progress." With luck, I might create a whole new art form. Every generation someone ought to come along and shake the field awake. Hemingway did it in his day and I could do it, too. Who knew? I might be the new Picasso of the pen!

When I finished my notes for the day, I grabbed a book I'd found in the garbage by the back door. The cover announced it had won the Pulitzer Prize for fiction. The foreword explained that it had been written by some poor slob who committed suicide shortly after writing it, because no one wanted to publish the damn thing. After his death, his mother dragged the manuscript around, begging anyone and everyone to read her son's "great" novel. Well someone finally did and discovered he was a genius. Terrific. A little late, but terrific.

I couldn't imagine Mom doing the same for me. If *I* dropped dead, the first thing she'd do is set fire to my room! The thought depressed me so, I couldn't read. I shoved the book under the bed (the place reserved for my paperbacks) and decided to go out. A long walk on Broadway was what I needed.

Mom stopped me at the door.

"You're not leaving the house looking like *that*."

I looked at myself in the hall mirror. The jeans were still respectable: only my knees stuck out. Sure, there was a tear in the rear end, but my back pocket covered that. The tee shirt only had some goulash on it: good for another week, at least.

"You're not walking around the neighborhood like that. Go change your clothes."

Weekends were the pits. I wanted it to be Monday, with Mom back in the butcher shop, off my back.

"I haven't any clothes. The roaches ate them."

"I wouldn't be surprised if you had *rats* in there, too." Mom grabbed her bag from the hook in the hall. "I'm not going through that mess of yours. Here's money, buy some decent pants. And a white shirt wouldn't hurt. The kind with buttons, Janci, remember those?"

"I've no time, Mom, I've—"

"Make time," she said, shoving the bills in my pocket, where they fell through the rip, onto the floor.

"Never mind. I'll stick the money in my sneaker."

"Do that. Shove it through the holes in the toes. If there's cash left, buy a new pair of sneakers, too."

Chapter 3

Everything has been written, except those things nobody wrote about. So I write them. . . . *E.H.*

Saturday on Broadway is great. During the week when I'm stuck in school, I always miss my ramblings through the neighborhood. The human parade keeps passing by while I'm imprisoned in that Bored-of-Education Vacuum, unable to witness it. It's a frustrating feeling, knowing the best things are happening when I'm powerless to record them. Six hours a day, the Boswell of Broadway is forced to scribble math equations while life seethes and teems outside.

Crossing the avenue, I noticed some construction along the Broadway malls. Parks Department workers had dug up the island to plant trees and flowers. Two guys sat on a bench alongside, watching.

"So what's this mean?"

"What else? The rents'll go up."

"No, maybe they're trying to kill us. Didn't someone say trees give out poison gases?"

"Only *you* give out poison gases, Sidney, so keep your mouth shut."

Passing the piles of earth stacked beside the gutter, I noticed an old lady, neatly dressed and prim. One of those sweet souls, overwhelmed by the city growing around her aging, infirm body, one who yearns for sweeter, gentler times. I wanted to ask her what she thought about the new beautification plan; certain she wouldn't voice such a jaded attitude. As I approached, the poor thing stepped right in a pothole. I lurched forward to help her, but she pushed me aside.

"Damn it," she shouted. "This city won't spend one red cent to fix the streets. But they spend a fortune for beauty, damned bastards!" Mumbling further curses under her breath, she kicked dirt into the park employee's face.

You can't make up dialogue like that! Naturally, I took out my pad to jot it down.

I'd only been out five minutes and already I'd collected some gems. It would be a good day.

I decided to buy the clothes before getting too involved. There was a line-up in the Army-Navy store, so I checked out The Gap. I grabbed the first jeans I saw. And a tee shirt with one of those dumb alligators sewn on. (I'd rip that off as soon as I got home.)

As I stood on line, I realized I'd picked the wrong

25

store. Beth Ann, from school, was waiting just in front of me.

Beth Ann has the hots for me, which she's made clear on more than one occasion. But I can't get excited about a girl who wears two rings in her nose. I'm afraid if I kissed her, we'd be looped together for life.

"John!" She smiled. "How're you doing?"

I blinked. Since I'd seen her last, Beth Ann had dyed her hair orange. It was a surprise.

"Just fine. How about you?"

"No complaints," she said, moistening her lips. "Not yet, anyway." She gave the statement a double entendre a cretin couldn't miss. "Did you do that composition for English?"

"Composition" . . . a real sixth grade term—probably the year Beth Ann's brain stopped functioning. Composition: the art of putting words together. Compose . . . compost . . . dung heap. Yeah, I guess I'd achieved that, all right!

I nodded.

"I'll bet it's intense," she said, breathing heavily. "You're the most intense person I know."

"Thanks, Beth Ann, same to you."

She shifted her weight from one high-heeled boot to another. "Yeah, that English class is a real trip."

Beth Ann was probably high on uppers all the time, so a visit to the toilet would be a big trip for her!

"Sure is," I agreed. "Holloway's a genius, without a doubt."

It was *her* turn to blink. The line of blue glop smeared above her eyes met the line of green glop smeared underneath them.

"You think so? I don't always get what he's saying."

"Maybe because you're under the desk most of the time."

"What's that?"

"A joke, Beth Ann."

"Oh." She giggled stupidly. "Listen, a bunch of us are hanging around the monument later. Wanna come?"

The Fireman's Monument on Riverside Drive is the meeting place for every spaced-out kid in the neighborhood. They drink beer, pop pills and wait for the cops to chase them away. Since none of the aforementioned prospects intrigued me, I was forced to decline.

"I'll be wearing this new sweater," she said as an added enticement. She held it up for me to see. It was an understated little number: red lips with a razor blade stuck through them.

"Real nice; it suits you."

"Thank you, Johnny."

The only thing I hate worse than being called Janos or Janci is being called Johnny.

"Excuse me," I said, throwing the clothes on the counter. "I've gotta go."

"You're not buying that shirt with the alligator? Bet you'd look sporty in it."

"Maybe. But I forgot. I'm a vegetarian."

* * *

Saved from the fate of having Beth Ann watch me take money from my sneaker, I moved on to the Salvation Army. On Saturdays, it's a lively joint. Personally, I preferred it when only the poor shopped there. Now it's the "in" place to find "in" clothes from the forties and fifties that people have thrown out, not knowing or caring they're back "in" again.

Young marrieds who can't afford new furniture poke around in there, too. But they're not the good material. The scuzzy deadbeats who blow their noses on the overcoats are far more interesting. Murphy also gets lots of street crazies. They wander in off Broadway, looking for a place to keep warm. There's always someone babbling to himself in back of the store or sitting on the second-hand furniture, eating junk retrieved from the garbage.

The eccentrics are best to observe: the ones who look like bums, but are actually just odd. Lots of them have college educations: former professors and everything, who've dropped out of the rat-race for various reasons. Unfortunately, they also haunt the bookshelves, so I've got to compete with them for the bargains.

One foot in the door, I could tell the crowd was running true to form. A woman dumped a pile of clothes on the counter as high as a mountain, while her five kids ran around the store screaming.

Two teenage girls were rummaging through a binful of vintage underwear, holding up grossly oversized girdles, then giggling.

And some old guy was in the corner, shouting, "Jesus died for you, Murphy. What are you doing for him?"

"Letting you live, fella. What have you got there?"

The old man shuffled over to the counter and thrust a pink umbrella in Murphy's face.

"It rained yesterday, Murphy. God sent rain and I got this umbrella from the stack over there."

"Yeah, so?"

"So I'm returning it. Pink's for a woman. I'm a man."

"Okay." Murphy sighed. "You want your money back. What'd I charge you?"

The old man looked indignant. "Nothing. I wouldn't buy a pink umbrella. You gave it to me. Now it's not raining, so I want to exchange it for something better."

Yeah, the crowd was running true to form.

I threw Murphy a wave. He nodded hello, running his fingers through his curly gray hair. Murph was a little guy, with rosy, elfin Irish cheeks, who managed to maintain a twinkle in his washed-out gray eyes: a wise old leprechaun, set loose among the jaded inmates of the city.

I think Murph noticed I frequented the place \solely\ to ransack the bookshelves, but he never asked me any questions. He had enough to deal with, without getting too personally involved with his "customers." I secretly suspect he thinks I'm a young junkie, reselling the books on the street for profit. I'd certainly never tell him I was a bonafide member of the middle class; he might think less of me.

Someday, I've plans to present him with a leather-bound, autographed, first-edition copy of my magnum opus, with a bookmark cleverly placed in the chapter describing La Salvation Boutique.

I ambled to the bookshelves and gave them the once-over: mainly tired old titles left over from last week. I spied cartons on the floor. Aha, new blood, not yet placed on the shelf. Sometimes, on lucky days, I can unearth someone's entire collection on one topic or author. One fateful day, I found all of Graham Greene . . . in hard cover yet . . . neatly stacked in a bottom box.

I get an uncanny sixth sense when I know something good is waiting for me, so I dug to the bottom, like it was a kid's grab bag. An interesting title poked out: *Voices from Behind Bars.* I'd never read anything by convicts, so it looked promising. As I grabbed for it, an immense tattooed hand reached in, too. Its scarred-up knuckles and filthy fingers instantly pushed my hand aside.

"I want that," said a voice I wouldn't dream of arguing with.

I looked up. The hand matched the face: cauliflower ear, broken nose, front teeth missing. The guy wore a pea jacket and a knit cap, the kind ex-cons always have in movies.

It didn't take long to figure out his personal interest in the book in question. Here was a genuine refugee from the slammer, the clink, the big house, the rock. Had he gone over the wall, blasted out or been paroled?

"How much they charge for books in here?"

"Real cheap. A quarter, maybe."

He nodded, leafing through the pages. "Yeah, I think I'll get me this." He tucked it in his coat pocket. "Whatsa matter?" he asked, noticing me staring. "Don'tcha think I can read?"

"Hey, sure you can. Looks like a good book, too. I wanted it myself."

"I saw it first," he said, making me feel he might produce a knife from his pocket any minute. "I got lotsa pals inside. Maybe one of 'em's wrote somethin' in here. They was always tryin' to make ya write down crap. Ya spend the day workin' in the laundry, then they expect ya to write down crap."

"Oh, are there writing programs in prison?" I asked (merely to be sociable).

As he stared at me, the scar over his eye made him look like he had two left eyebrows. "How'd ya know I was a con? I got it stamped on me or what?"

Of course he did, but catch me telling him!

"Guess it was the book," I explained.

"Oh yeah," he said, patting the pocket he'd placed it in. "What's a kid like you interested in this stuff for? You thinkin' to write down crap, too?"

"Well, I'm interested in writing," I admitted. "And people; interesting ones."

"Ever been inside the slammer?"

"Me? No."

"They got lotsa characters in there, for sure. My pal, Georgy, what's got sent up for life, he's real interestin'. I talked to 'im all the time, till they put 'im in solitary. Bet his stories ain't nothin' like this book. I got a few myself."

"I'd like to hear them sometimes," I said off-handedly.

"You bet." He shrugged, then moved down the aisle to fumble through a stack of chipped cups and plates.

Damn. The only decent book in the box and the Dead End Kid had grabbed it. Bet he did have great stories to tell, though. Could he be valuable material?

As I thought about it, I found myself staring straight into the buttons of a tape recorder. It was hidden on the corner shelf: one of those great super spy jobs that tucks in a pocket. A battery-powered bonanza.

I realized my awkward problems with human research had ended. With a tiny tape recorder, I needn't resort to hanging off the roof or sticking a glass to my ear to hear specific conversations. I could bring it everywhere; get down conversations without anyone noticing. I could go anywhere. Record anyone. My realm would expand to the whole community.

"Hey Murphy, what do you want for this?"

"Sorry kid, can't give it to you for less than twenty-five."

Twenty-five bucks! It would cost *two hundred* in the store.

Murphy must've misinterpreted my blank stare of disbelief as poverty.

"Okay, make it twenty. It works real good. There's a tape in it already. I tried it out myself."

I curled my toes around the bills resting in my

sneaker. How could I pass up such a bargain? But if I returned home without new clothes, there'd be hell to pay.

"It's a deal. Got any decent jeans upstairs?"

"Sure, lots of them."

"Okay, hold this for me while I check."

I went upstairs and examined the racks. There were two pairs of jeans that would probably fit. A little faded, but I'd tell Mom it was the "pre-washed" look. I found a sweat shirt in decent condition, then threw in a white shirt for good measure. That'd make Mom happy.

I checked the shoe rack in the corner: only a pair of purple joggers. Too big: size fifteen. On my already huge feet they looked like clown shoes, but who cared? Why hadn't I thought of this before? Next time Mom insisted I buy clothes, I'd siphon off some cash for books and other necessities. What a deal.

"Hey kid, ya really gonna wear those things?"

It was my Dead End friend, trying on a jacket in the corner.

"Sure, why not?"

"No skin off my nose, but they look like clown shoes, ya know."

He turned to glance at himself in the full-length mirror. The jacket was a black and white pinstripe from the forties, which made him look like Edward G. Robinson. Apparently, he was trading in his prison attire for a proper gangster uniform.

"What d'ya think? Now that I'm out, I wanna look respectable."

"Very nice," I said, trying to hide my amusement.

As I stared at the guy, whom Damon Runyon would've kindly classified as "a broken-down lug," it came to me at last that I was face-to-face with my golden opportunity. Shades of Truman Capote! I had found my very own criminal. What a dope I was! I'd almost let him slip away, and he was undoubtedly the "colorful character" I'd been waiting to be inspired by.

Why had he been in prison? With any luck, it might have been for an ax murder or two. But I wasn't greedy. I'd settle for a bank robber or a member of the Mafia. Within moments, Fate had supplied me with a bonafide criminal *and* the machine with which to record his life story. By my calculations, if I bought the clothes, I'd still have several dollars left. Would that be enough to entice him to "spill his guts"?

"Listen, would you like to make some money?"

He shook his head, wiped his nose and shrugged. "Listen kid, I'm clean, ya know."

Guess he thought I wanted him to slit a throat . . . rub someone out.

"Those stories you mentioned before. I'd like to hear them, get some down on tape. I'll pay you ten bucks."

He seemed suspicious. "Ten smackers, just ta hear me talk. What's the catch? You some kinda prevert?"

"It's research for a book I'm doing."

"No kidding, research, huh? Well it's okay by me. Ya want I should start talkin' now?" He stuck out his chin, fingering the lapels of the pinstripe, as if preparing to appear on camera.

"Not here," I said, writing down my address. "Monday maybe. Around four? Can you make it?"

I handed him the paper. "You ain't put down no name. Ain't we gonna introduce ourselves?"

"John. John Sandor," I said, holding out my hand.

"Clifford," he said, pulverizing my fingers.

I winced. "Hello, Mr. Clifford."

"Not mister, that's my first name. Karlbach's the last. Call me Cliff."

"Okay Cliff, then it's a deal?"

"Sure. Monday at four. I ain't goin' nowhere."

I grabbed my pile of clothes and started down the stairs.

"Hold it," he shouted. "Don't expect me ta tell ya nothin' about that bank job back in '78. Two pals made off with that one and never got pinched. I got principles, ya know."

His convict code impressed me.

"Okay. I'd rather hear about your life in prison, anyway."

"That's what I figured," he grumbled. "There's always someone wantin' to write down crap."

The deal finalized, I set about paying Murphy. With Cliff's cash aside for Monday, I was still five bucks ahead.

Not a bad Saturday afternoon.

* * *

Chapter 4

_____

These stories are mostly about things and people that people won't care about. All right, sooner or later, as the wheel keeps turning, I will have ones that they will like. . . . E.H.

Everything was going great. At home, I palmed off my second-hand purchases on Mom. She made a funny face, but bought that "pre-washed" garbage. Of course, she was amazed I'd chosen purple joggers. Luckily, she chalked it up to bad taste. (Parents are always prepared to believe the worst about a guy, anyway.) But her face lit up when she saw the white shirt. She practically patted me on the head!

I hid the tape recorder in my desk drawer, looking forward to using it on Monday when Cliff came over. Mom would be at the butcher shop until after eight, so that was cool. And *I* planned to cool it in the building the rest of the weekend, steering clear of the Mancussos.

I spent Sunday in my room, typing up chapters of *The Sun Also Rises,* then sorting through my books. Browsing through their pages began setting my brain in motion. I wrote down various topics to ask Cliff about.

What great material: a pathetic ex-con, a destitute loner, shunned by society, now back in its midst. What changes had he observed in the city since his incarceration? What cruel, inhuman experiences had turned him to a life of crime?

Somehow, I knew if I could zero in on Cliff's story, I'd have a main character worthy of my book. He'd be my precious gem in a ring encrusted with smaller stones. Yeah, Cliff in the foreground, with Murphy and the Mancussos, maybe, as background characters. Or perhaps I'd use the Mancussos to suggest domestic violence while Cliff represented a greater social violence.

Whatever, I'd work it out step by step. I was sitting on a powder keg of creativity, just waiting to blow!

Monday, I daydreamed through most of my classes, anxious for my ex-con encounter. When Holloway called for the essays, I'd almost forgotten my scathing one. In a better mood now, I regretted having written it. Hell, handing in no paper was sure to get me an F, so it didn't matter.

Passing my paper down the row, Beth Ann whispered from in front of me.

"I had a hard time choosing," she confided. "Which kind of pencil, I mean. There's the plain yellow kind and the ones with the hole in the middle."

The suspense of her choice was killing me.

"Anyway," she continued, "I decided—"

"No talking back there, Sandor," Holloway shouted.

"Who me? I wasn—"

"Yes, yes, I know. You're *never* doing anything."

A chorus of stifled giggles round-robined the room. The pompous pinhead!

"Give me that," I mumbled, grabbing back my essay from Beth Ann. I quickly red-penciled the top of it: ATTENTION MR. HOLLOW-HEADED HOLLOWAY, then passed it down the row. And to think I'd almost begun to regret what I'd written. I wish I could be around when he read the damn thing!

After school, I rushed home, put the tape recorder on the kitchen table and placed one of Dad's bottles of scotch beside it. My guest would probably need a few fingers of booze to loosen up.

Cliff arrived at four o'clock, sharp. He was wearing the old pinstripe and had his hair slicked down with some vile-smelling grease. He must've smeared it on his shoes, too, which seemed to have attracted great balls of lint.

"How about a belt first," I offered, holding up the scotch bottle.

"No thanks, bum stomach. Got any milk?"

I poured us both a glass, then switched on the recorder. "Cliff, I thought we'd start with the first time you were arrested."

"Damn, is that a Maryellis?" he shouted, staring at Mom's plant by the kitchen sink.

"A what?"

"I mean amaryllis," he explained, walking over to finger the petals. "Never get the names right, but she's a beauty."

"Yeah, real pretty. Listen, tell me when—"

"And hyacinths," he said excitedly. "Begonias, even a gardenia." He started walking around the kitchen. "Get morning sun here, right? No wonder those suckers are bloomin' like crazy. I tried keepin' a few plants inside my cell, but they didn't make it. They knew they was prisoners and gave up."

Since the interview wasn't going as planned, I decided to go with the flow.

"When did you first get interested in flowers, Cliff? Prison?"

"Na, when I was a kid. Had my own windowbox; the only one in Hell's Kitchen. I pulled my first job, hopin' to get enough dough to open a flower store. So that's the breaks, right?"

Cliff was starting to roll. After several glasses of milk, I'd managed to record a mess of stuff. What a hard-luck guy. Cliff's affinity for flowers hadn't prevented him from breaking lots of bones in his day. One particular broken nose belonged to a cop. That assault put him in prison a long time. When he got out, he drifted around, unable to hold a job. He wanted something working with flowers, but didn't look the type. That's when he got the brilliant idea to hold up a store, so he could own one of his own. It was back and forth, in and out of the clink, after that.

During his many incarcerations, he'd accumulated a cauliflower ear, a broken nose, a ruptured spleen and several broken ribs. He'd also lopped off part of a finger in the prison laundry's mangler and developed an ulcer. Apparently, none of this had deadened his joy at seeing a flower take root and bloom.

What a fantastic allegory. Mr. Clifford Karlbach was the personification of the city: hard, tough and scarred on the outside, yet sensitive to beauty. With Cliff as my foundation, I could build a portrait of the city: cruel, vicious, yet beautiful. A Studs Terkel, Carl Sandburg depiction of the Upper West Side . . . a Hemingwayesque masterpiece!

"Your machine stopped," he said, guzzling down his fourth glass of milk. "Guess that means it's time ta go. Where's my ten bucks?"

The time had flown and I had no more tape left. But I couldn't let Cliff leave, just as I was conceptionalizing my format.

"We've only begun," I argued. "There's much more I want to know."

He shrugged. "Listen kid, I don't like talkin' about the joint, ya know. I'm out now. Maybe not for long, but let's forget it, okay. Just gimme my dough like we agreed."

Guess I couldn't blame Cliff for not wanting to dwell on the past. The prison stories he'd told were graphic . . . rotten food, rotten prisoners, rotten guards. It was all the stuff I'd thought I wanted to hear, but now it sounded like something from a cheap novel. Cliff's love of nature was what fascinated me. How had he managed to nurture it all those years behind bars?

"Can't we talk more?" I asked, giving him the money. "I'd like to hear more about your interest in flowers."

He gave me a steely-eyed look as he tucked the cash inside the pinstripe pocket. "You serious or what?"

"Sure I am."

"Listen, I ain't ashamed of it or nothin'. I told ya right out straight, didn't I? Sure, a person who can't smile at a plant ain't no better'n a piece a meat. Ya shoulda seen those big apes in the stir. I had 'em actin' like babies when they started seein' them seeds come up."

"You grew plants in prison?"

"Some. The warden gave me a piece a the exercise yard for a garden."

"You had a *garden* in prison?"

"No big deal, but nice enough. Hollyhocks, the tall jobs, Impatiens, the short stuff. And a small patch a lemon something. I made 'em grow real good, but I can't say those lousy names on the packets. Makes ya feel like a dope, ya know. Listen kid, I gotta go. My parole officer's waitin'. It's been swell meetin' ya, Johnny. Keep your nose clean."

"Cliff, I'm out of cash right now. When I get some, will you come back and tell me more about your garden?"

"Aw kid, I don't want money ta gab about flowers. It's good just thinkin' about 'em, ya know. Why didn't ya say that's what ya was interested in, insteada wastin' time talkin' about the stir? Bet ya had me pegged right off, huh? These mitts are a giveaway."

He extended his huge hands to show me his fingernails. (I'd assumed the dirt underneath was plain old dirt, but I guess it was actually earth dirt.)

"Yeah." He laughed. "A dead giveaway."

"So you'll come again?"

"Sure, why not. Know anything about compost? Never mind, I know it all."

I hesitated to admit I wasn't interested in gardening per se, merely as character background.

"Where are you staying? In the neighborhood?"

"Yeah, I got a room a few blocks away. Got a job, too. Dishwasher, four nights a week."

I glanced at his filthy hands again.

"Oh, I ain't started yet. By next week, these fingers'll be as white as that flower. Those plants do ya proud, Johnny. What d'ya put in the soil?"

"A bit of this, a bit of that," I said blankly.

"I get it." He nodded. "A secret, eh? Well it's workin' for ya, so keep it up. Lemme give ya some advice though, kid. Don't be greedy with your secrets. Gardeners gotta share, ya know? But you're green yet, you'll learn. Gotta go now, kid. It's been fun. Not the crap about prison, but the rest. Want I should come by tomorrow?"

"At four? That'll be great."

He threw down a final glass of milk for the road, smiled at the plants and left.

I spent the whole evening in my room. I bypassed the cold tongue platter Mom had left for me in the fridge. (Sometimes I think she plants beauts like that in there on purpose!) Instead, I made three cheese sandwiches, took them to my room and thought. After my folks got home, Mom banged on the door several times, but I ignored her.

I played Cliff's tape over and over again, getting acquainted with the mug-faced lug in love with flowers. I hadn't realized how my research had been crying out for a character like this.

If only I could discover a couple more treasures like him: poor souls on the lowest rung of society, trying to maintain a semblance of humanity. Then I'd surely have a trilogy. Yeah, a writing triptych that could pull me in a Pulitzer while I was still a teenager!

But where could I find other rough gems like Cliff? The street crazies were in a world of their own. A shopping bag lady, maybe? Or the Onion Bag Man? Na, with all his "Quarter please" begging, he was probably a millionaire by now.

Leaving the building the next morning, it suddenly came to me. That's the time the maids begin arriving.

Most tenants aren't ritzy enough for live-in help, but lots employ nine-to-fivers. Illegal aliens, mostly. I've observed them and noticed the furtive look in their eyes; always checking over their shoulder, fearful of discovery. Without a green card, they can be booted out of the country if someone discovers them working here. Maybe they're also scared they'll be arrested for stealing some soap or for not washing out a mop properly. Yet, they're all part of the city's working underground. Without them, middle class life as we know it would grind to a halt.

That morning, I saw the piggy-faced girl on the third floor who works for Mrs. Reiss. She doesn't share that scared expression and I'd wondered why.

Mrs. Reiss works and needs someone to polish, clean and generally maintain the humungous collection of bad-taste, kitschy junk she's collected for years. When I was twelve, I sometimes sat for her dog and nearly went crazy wandering through her maze of Chinese urns, garish rugs and whoopy cushions. Her dog probably did go nuts; he's dead now. I bet he overdosed on Alpo to get out of the place.

Anyway, this girl has the job of keeping things in shape. She's about twenty, I guess. Unlike most illegals, she's not from the Islands or Latin America. Judging from the few words I've heard her mumble in the elevator, I think she's from Upper Slombovia or something. Probably one of those countries the Russians stamped out.

There I was on my way to school, really engrossed in my plans for my trilogy, when I slammed the lobby door behind me. I didn't see her trying to rush through before it closed. I heard a shreik and turned around. She'd slipped on the rug, spilled her packages and bumped her head. Naturally, I felt like hell and helped her up. She smiled, trying to rearrange the ring of braids on her head. With her chubby, rosy cheeks, she should've been herding sheep on a mountain somewhere, or dancing the polka with bosoms flying.

Then it came to me: Cliff, who should've been poking around Mary-Quite-Contrary's garden, and Heidi here . . . what a combination.

"Are you okay?" I asked, picking up her packages.

She smiled. "Yah."

(Good, she spoke English.)

"Sorry, didn't see you."

"Yah." She smiled again.

"What's your name?"

"Yah." She nodded this time.

(Guess she didn't speak English, after all.)

"My name's John."

"Grendel."

(Now we were making progress.)

"Do you need any help?"

"Grendel."

All her nodding and smiling began making her look like a wind-up toy. I tried remembering the few phrases of Hungarian I knew; assuming all European languages have some similarity. But I wasn't sure what I was saying. It may've been: in-my-father's-house-there-is-a-table. Then again, it could've been: go-to-the-window-and-see-the-water.

By some miracle, she picked something comprehensible from it. Suddenly, her face lit up and she began babbling in a mother tongue still unknown to me.

Fascinating. If she didn't speak English, how'd she survive in the city? Was there, perhaps, a small secret band of other Upper Slombovians to come to her aid? I had to find out.

As I followed her to the elevator, she continued talking, nodding, smiling. I kept nodding, too; pretending to understand every word. When we got to Mrs. Reiss's door, she asked me in. At least I *think* that's what she did.

She pulled at my arm and nodded, "Yah?"

"Yah . . . I mean, okay. Just for a minute."

Mrs. Reiss's apartment was as unbelievable as ever. I recognized the moosehead in the hall, but the bearskin rug and the Napoleon lamp were new additions.

Grendel led me to the dining room, practically pushing me into a chair. As she unpacked her grocery bag I discovered she knew yet another English word . . . Coca-Cola. There were several six-packs in the bag. Flipping the lid, she handed me one, as foam spit from the top. (Yes, I could definitely see her in some Bavarian beer hall, with snow-capped mountains in the distance.)

"Is this your breakfast?" I asked.

"Yah. Coca-Cola."

"Are those the only words you know?"

"Yah. Coca-Cola."

"How do you know what work to do? How do you talk to Mrs. Reiss?"

At the mention of Mrs. Reiss, Grendel jumped up, ran to the kitchen and returned with a book. A kiddie picture book called *Mommy Works,* with drawings of a woman doing household chores. By each picture, someone (obviously Mrs. Reiss) had drawn a clock, its hands pointing to a time. The woman doing laundry had the clock pointing to ten, the woman sleeping had it at eleven, and so on.

"I see. You just follow the pictures?"

Grendel smiled and nodded.

There were no pictures of "mommy" drinking Coke, so I assumed that was left to Grendel's discretion.

Suddenly I felt uncomfortable, alone in the apartment with a grinning peasant girl, making great cow-eyes at me. But I felt sorry for her, too. Old Mrs. Reiss probably paid her nothing an hour, time-and-a-half for overtime.

"Where do you live?"

She answered with several "yahs," then opened me another Coke.

"No," I explained, "live . . . house . . . where's your house?" I flipped through her book, hoping to find a picture of a building. I found one of "mommy" making the bed. "Sleep. Where do you sleep?"

She looked at the picture, looked back at me, then blushed. Then she laughed; a big-bosomed chuckle that nearly knocked me off my seat. Taking my arm, she led me to a small room off the kitchen, with a cot in the corner.

Now I understood. Grendel wasn't a nine-to-fiver after all. She *lived* with Mrs. Reiss.

"I see. You sleep here?"

Grendel nodded too, but I felt we weren't talking about the same thing!

I tried my feeble Hungarian again, but that made things worse. Grendel was coming on to me, for sure, and I was getting nervous as hell. I had the awful feeling that in another minute she'd have me pinned to the bed!

"I've gotta go now," I said, heading for the door. But all that Coke Grendel guzzled must've given her super strength. Next thing I knew, she'd slammed me against the wall and was kissing me. Hard. So hard, I thought she'd rip off my lips.

At first I was surprised, of course, but then I got angry. How many other unsuspecting souls had she lured in here with promises of unlimited Coca-Cola? Delivery boys? Window washers? Meter readers? Bet I wasn't the first.

Then I realized where I'd heard her name before. In Beowulf, Grendel is the rapacious monster who comes every night to carry off a feudal knight. Damn, I could add a stanza or two to the epic poem. How'd it go again? . . . "With his grip he grappled the gruesome Grendel."

Not a bad idea. But I suspected this modern-day Grendel's grip was stronger than mine. So I ran like hell, instead. Really. I practically fell over the bearskin rug, trying to escape.

Grendel, not understanding the subtlety of my reaction, chased after me. She placed a hammerlock around my neck, making me suspect her time off from mopping was spent studying wrestling.

I managed to free myself and grab the doorknob.

"Goodbye," I shouted.

As she finally realized I didn't want to stay, her face grew sad. I had the awful feeling she was about to cry. Maybe she'd thought all my pushing and protests was a romantic cat-and-mouse game.

"Listen, I'm sorry about the mix-up. I'll bet you're not an illegal alien at all. You see, I was doing research."

Damn, why bother? She couldn't understand a word. Those big cow-eyes began watering, so I decided to leave before they flooded the floor.

Slamming the door behind me, I took a deep breath. Just my luck, Mr. Abernathy was coming from his apartment down the hall. I stood awkwardly, praying the elevator would come quickly.

Abernathy smiled. "Good morning, John."

He was a weasel-faced little guy, who always carried an umbrella. He lived alone, never had visitors, kept strange hours and talked to himself. I'd recently put him on my list of candidates for "research," because I secretly suspected he was a weirdo. The kind of guy who probably keeps a blow-up plastic woman in his room!

"Lovely morning," he said, following me into the elevator. Then he smiled again.

It was a furtive half-smile, which seemed to imply something. Had the incident with the water glass gotten around the building? I wondered. Yeah, there was definitely something in his manner that seemed to suggest we were kindred spirits.

It all became clear when I caught a glimpse of myself in the lobby mirror. Grendel had smeared lipstick all over my damn face. Now I *really* looked like a clown . . . shoes and face to match. Terrific.

Old Abernathy gave me a sly, fellow-pervert-type grin. "Have a good day, John," he said, swinging his umbrella in the air. As he reached the lobby door, I heard him laugh under his breath.

Well, it was my own fault for being greedy. I should've been satisfied with finding a great character like Cliff, instead of jumping the gun, looking for others. For the moment, my idea of a trilogy flew out the window as I scratched Grendel from my list of research possibilities. I hoped I'd never see her piggy-face again.

Yeah, one idea at a time was enough for me. After all, Flaubert spent ages fooling around with *Madame Bovary*. Sometimes, he'd work on one sentence all day, so I could certainly concentrate on Cliff awhile.

I was glad I'd escaped Grendel's grip, but the *gruesome* encounter had left me very late for school, especially by the time I'd cleaned up. Lipstick doesn't come off all that easy. By the time I arrived, then waited in the principal's office for a late slip, it'd be lunchtime. Hardly worth bothering.

Instead, I walked up to Broadway and spent my left-over cash on tapes. Then I went back home and pounded out a few chapters of Hemingway on the old typewriter. I made myself some food, then waited for Clifford to stop by. He arrived at four sharp, carrying a package wrapped in florist's paper.

"This is for you, Johnny."

Unwrapping it, I discovered it was a fuzzy-leafed plant.

"Catnip," he explained. "You're doin' so good with flowers, I thought ya'd like to try somethin' different."

"You shouldn't have," I said awkwardly.

"Aw, forget it. I got to feelin' real lousy about takin' your dough yesterday." He took the plant and placed it lovingly on the windowsill. "Keep'er wet and she'll grow real nice."

"I'll do that," I said, switching on the tape recorder. "Are we ready to roll?"

"Whatever you say, Johnny. Pardon my gettin' per-sonal, but how old are ya?"

"Sixteen."

"Hell, I started earlier. Twelve's when I got hooked. We lived in this cold water flat, see, with nothin' outside the window but garbage and drunken bums. Then one day, I seen this flower, growin' right up through the street. It knocked me out! The only flowers I seen before was in church when my old man died. But this was growin' right outside the front door, next to beer cans and junk. Guess I adopted it or somethin'. I banged away at the concrete, givin' it some room to breathe, then I started waterin' it. It did real good, too, until some lug threw a crate out the window and crushed it."

A faint quiver entered Cliff's voice as he continued discussing his first flower . . . his first love, actually . . . and its untimely death. After its demise, he began growing things on the sly: first, seeds in paper cups, then a few bulbs. He'd steal the money from his mother, then blow it in the gardening section of Woolworths.

And thus, Cliff's strange life combining horticulture and crime began. Violence, too. Naturally, the street toughs ribbed him about his hobby, so he was forced to break many bones in their bodies! Street fights led to cop fights and a life in and out of prison. Strange he still maintained such a great love for plants, when they were the cause of all his trouble.

His eyes lit up when he began talking about his prison garden. He glowed with pride, as if discussing his children. In a way I guess they were: wife, children, family, *everything* to him.

"Winter's the roughest time in stir. Nothin's growin' outside. That's when I tried bringin' some flowers in the cell. The shock killed 'em. Plants can't grow with bars around 'em. People can't, neither."

"That's a very profound thought, Cliff."

He shrugged. "Sure, profound. I only hope those lugs

ain't killin' my petunias. They don't know a weed from a watermelon."

"Why not go up on visiting day and take a look?"

"Not a bad idea, Johnny. My irises should be up soon. Maybe I'll see how they're doin'.

We talked some more, until the tape ran out. I was ready to slip another one in the machine, but Cliff said he had to go.

"Gotta be at the joint soon," he explained. "First time on the job."

"The restaurant?"

"Well, they got food there if that's what ya mean. But I wouldn't touch the stuff."

"Can you come back tomorrow?"

"Don't know. They ain't worked out all my hours. But I'll see ya sometime soon."

Cliff gave the flowers a goodbye glance and left with a melancholy look on his face. What a strange, sad guy.

But what great book material. I couldn't wait to start typing it. I took the tape recorder to my room. And the plant, too. Mom would think something was up if she discovered I'd bought *catnip*. She'd probably start rummaging through my room, trying to uncover a hidden feline. I could almost hear her. "Cats? You're keeping cats now, Janos? Roaches aren't enough?"

Where should I put the damn plant? If I stuck it on my desk, I'd have to water it. Would that mean the beginning of a lifelong involvement with fauna? Would I take a "leaf" from Cliff's book, traveling down the botanical road to degradation? Better not take chances. I hid the plant under the bed. If cats got drunk on it, maybe roaches would, too.

I cultivated the thought: one of Archy's cousins, high as a kite, weaving around the room, with a telltale strand of leaf on its antenna.

Damn, I was wiped out. My encounter with Grendel had left me exhausted. I zonked out on the bed and fell asleep. Several hours later, I heard Mom banging on the door.

I rolled over and went back to sleep.

Chapter 5

Public psycho-analyzing of living writers is most certainly
an invasion of privacy. . . . E.H.

I wasn't anxious to go to school the next day. Holloway's wrath regarding my essay was sure to hit the fan.
Luckily, he was absent, so our encounter was postponed.
We had a substitute, which means we did absolutely nothing. All subs can do is say, "Take out a book and read." I
made some further notes on Cliff, but it bugged me that
I didn't know when I'd be seeing him again. I hated to
waste valuable time.

Before lunch, I discovered my math teacher was also
absent. That would mean a whole day in school wasted,
too. I decided to cut afternoon classes and do something
worthwhile.

I bummed around the neighborhood, hoping fate would once again steer me in some promising direction. Stopping in McDonald's for a hamburger, I found myself staring at the old black man who mops up. A little boy was staring at him, too. The old guy just finished giving everything a once-over, when this kid dumps his paper cup of ice cubes on the clean floor. Maybe he wanted to see how quickly the old man reacted. Within seconds, he was back with his mop, sloshing it around. Then the kid took another cup and did the same thing. The poor guy cleaned that up, too, without blinking. Guess lots of people's lives are spent cleaning up after others.

That made me think of garbage men: the guys who keep the city running by disposing of our refuse. Maybe one of *them* might have an interesting slant on city life. If I were lucky, I might discover another Cliff: a closet poet or painter. It would mean interviewing lots of garbage men, but maybe it would be worth it.

I rolled the possibility around on my walk home. Unfortunately, the garbage had already been collected. I knew, because half of it was strewn along the sidewalk. Was this a definite statement by our noble sanitation engineers? Was that how they vented their resentment of the job? Or was it, perhaps, a humanitarian philosophy? Take some, but leave enough for others.

My weighty brooding regarding garbage suddenly flew from my head when I opened the apartment door. To my surprise, Mom and Dad were seated at the kitchen table, awaiting my arrival. From the expressions on their faces, they hadn't taken time off from the store just to share my company. Something was up, and it wasn't good.

"Sit down, Janos," said Dad. (It was an order, not an invitation.)

"How was school?" asked Mom. (I noted the sarcastic tone in her voice.)

"Okay, nothing special."

Then she pounced. "How could it be? You weren't there!"

"Sure I was, this morning."

"Not this afternoon. Not yesterday!"

My truancy discovered, I tried explaining. "There was a sub in English, so I. . . ."

"Do you know *why* there was a sub?" she asked, frowning so hard her eyes turned to slits. "Because Mr. Holloway practically dropped dead yesterday. Do you know *when* that happened, Janos? After he read that story of yours! If you'd been in school, you would've known that little fact. The poor man spent his lunch hour in the teachers' room, correcting English papers. When he got to yours, he choked on his sandwich! Thank God another teacher was there to give him the whatsis."

"The Heimlich maneuver," Dad interjected.

"That's the one. Without that, you would've been a *murderer*. Is that what you want, Janos? To kill that poor teacher?"

The idea was drastic, but not without its pleasant aspects.

"All I did was write his lousy essay. Where'd you hear all this junk, anyway?"

"The principal called my store this afternoon," said Dad. "He wanted to know why you weren't in school. Then Mr. Holloway called. I was cutting up a nice chicken for Mrs. Ungar at the time. I nearly lost a thumb! That poor man said he's thinking of leaving teaching, all because of kids like you."

"Did he give you that pearls-before-swine garbage?" I asked. "He's been saying that for twenty years. In all that time, he's never thrown a pearl in anyone's direction. Certainly not a *cultured* one!"

"Look at my face," said Mom somberly. "I'm not giggling, am I, Janos? No, I'm not going to. You think you only have to say something clever and things'll be okay. String a few words together and that's it. Not this time; it's too serious."

"C'mon, Mom, you know what a nerd Holloway is. Okay, I'll write him another essay; a good one this time. I'm sorry I cut class and skipped school, but I had things on my mind."

"And we know who it is!" said Dad. "Mr. Abernathy was in this morning for flank steak. I nearly lost *another* thumb!"

Abernathy? Damn, he didn't tell Dad about gruesome Grendel, did he? Obviously, he had.

"Dad, it's not the way you think."

"It never is. I remember the first time I. . . ."

Mom flashed him a look that would have cut through steel. "That's not the kind of talk we need, Joszef. You did that when he was fourteen. Things are serious now and need plain talk. So tell me, Janci, when and why'd you start fooling around with that housekeeper? She's years older than you. Mr. Abernathy says she can't even speak English. It's wrong to take advantage. . . ."

"*Advantage?* I never touched her, I *couldn't.*"

Dad looked concerned. "What do you mean, you *couldn't,* son?"

"I mean I wouldn't. I didn't want to."

"Then why'd you go to her apartment?" asked Mom. "*Alone,* when you should've been in school. And don't tell me it was *research.* I may be uneducated, but I'm not stupid."

What could I say? Mom had already knocked the wind from my perfectly legitimate excuse. It *was* research, pure and simple, but she'd never believe that now.

"I wanted to *talk* to her."

"With lipstick on your face?" asked Dad.

Clearly, Abernathy hadn't spared one damn detail!

"Look, son," said Dad, with a boys-will-be-boys tone. "You're only young once, but this isn't right."

By now, I figured the best thing was to admit what I hadn't done. It was the only way out.

"You're right, Dad. I promise I'll never see her again."

I thought that would put an end to the discussion,

but I was wrong. Solemnly, Dad rose from the kitchen chair, fiddled with his moustache, then said, "All right. Now we'd better discuss the real *serious* problem."

What the hell else? I wondered. They'd already dredged up everything I'd done for two days.

Dad switched from solemn to morose. "You'd better bring in the evidence, Anna."

Mom nodded and left the room. Waiting for her return, I felt I was about to face a firing squad. I was right. When Mom got back, I got it with both barrels!

She placed my tape recorder on the table, and next to it, my catnip plant. Then Mom and Dad both sat down, placing their arms across their chests: Supreme Court judges, minus the black robes.

I stared down at the objects Mom'd taken from my room. She had her nerve, snooping around. Yeah, I could be indignant, too.

"Well?" they asked.

"Well?" I said blankly, not knowing what they were driving at.

"We want an *explanation*."

"Okay. That's a recorder and that's a plant. Can I go now?"

"Sit down!" Dad bellowed, so loud I thought he'd blow his top. "That's a two hundred dollar tape recorder, Janos. *Two hundred bucks!* A lot of money for someone who doesn't have it. Someone who doesn't *work*. Someone who goofs off in school . . ."

"And locks himself in his room," Mom added. "I banged on your door for an hour last night. You were passed out."

"Someone who's passed out half the time," Dad continued. "Know how much meat I have to sell to make two hundred profit? How many chicken livers and calves' brains?"

"Joszef, no shop talk; not now. Our son's becoming a *criminal.*"

Maybe I was dense, but I didn't get it.

"A criminal, that's right," agreed Dad, getting back on track. "Janos'll never have to worry about the fine art of boning out. He's found an easier way to make money; and get high on the deal!" He grabbed the plant from the table and shook it in front of my face, until the leaves started falling off. "High as a kite, right, Janos? No wonder you don't give a damn about school or anything else. How many more of these have you got hidden? Where do you keep them . . . in the basement . . . on the roof?"

As I stood with my mouth hanging open, Mom beginning to cry, and the veins in Dad's forehead popping out purple, the whole stupid mess became graphically clear.

Marijuana! My folks thought I was smoking, growing and dealing pot!

It would've been laughable, if I wasn't in such trouble.

Mom and Dad obviously didn't know what marijuana looked like. Any fuzzy-leaved plant hidden under a guy's bed was a likely candidate. Why else would it be under the bed in the first place? And it neatly explained so much . . . my truancy, zonking out, fooling around . . . the expensive recorder I couldn't afford unless I was doing something illegal.

Getting my folks mad about Holloway wasn't cool. Having them think I had the hots for Grendel was worse. But they couldn't think I was an addict; that was *too* much.

There was nothing for it, but to tell the truth.

"Look, you're off-base here," I said, eager to straighten things out. "That's a catnip plant. It's a gift from an ex-con I met in the Salvation Army, where I bought my purple shoes."

Fool that I am, I thought that'd settle the matter. Instead, Dad turned a dangerous coronary shade of red.

"I've never hit him before, Anna, but—".

"No, Joszef, I'm calling the doctor."

Dad did look like he was having a heart attack.

"What's the number, Mom, *I'll* call."

"The doctor's not for him," said Mom, handing Dad a glass of water. As he gulped it down, the color began to drain from his face. "I'm calling Dr. Epstein for *you,* Janos. I want you to see him right away."

"Epstein? He's a *pediatrician.* I haven't been there in years."

"Well, you're going now. We've no psychiatrist, so Epstein'll check you out. He's known you since you were born. Maybe he can tell us why you've turned into . . .

I don't know what you've turned into. But in the meantime, I'm getting rid of *this*." Mom picked up the plant as if it were contaminated, holding it gingerly with two fingers. "What do the police do with these things, Joszef, burn them?"

"Flush it down the toilet," he said.

I'm glad Cliff wasn't around to witness the death of his innocent herb!

At ten thirty the next morning, I was in Dr. Epstein's waiting room. Mom escorted me there personally . . . *after* she'd been to school to speak to the principal . . . *after* she'd assured Mr. Holloway he'd have my written apology . . . and *after* I'd endured a twenty-minute lecture on the evils of drugs.

I was a quivering, lifeless mass of jelly by the time she dumped me in the outer office. Mom's hot Magyar blood had boiled up and she was in control.

"After you leave here, you go right to school, understand, Janos?"

It was both embarrassing and frustrating to be reduced to an emotional ten-year-old. Sitting in a waiting room of babies and runny-nosed kids didn't help, either.

Mom gave me my final words of warning. "Behave yourself!" Then she slammed the door behind her and went to work.

Every damn mother in the room began to stare at me, some nervously clutching their infants. Obviously, I was abnormal. I contemplated counting my toes, sucking my thumb or drooling, not wanting to deny the good ladies a good show. Luckily, mine was the next name called, so I hightailed it into old Epstein's office.

The smells and surroundings brought back memories of a childhood filled with measles, chicken pox, fractures and fevers. Or as Oscar Wilde put it: "a life crowded with incident." Through it all, Epstein was there, with splints, ear-prodders, tongue-depressors, needles and hammers. As a kid, the place struck terror into me: The Horror Chamber of Dr. Epstein—over which he presided with the iciest hands in town. He must've stuck them in the freezer before examining each patient. I remember the cold, hard strip of paper he'd stretch out on the examining table. Finished with his tortures, I'd stand up, he'd roll the sheet down, rip it off and throw it in the trash. It made me feel contaminated or something. Then he'd hand me a lollipop, always stale. The cellophane stuck to my teeth and caught in my throat.

And he always wore the same suit: a gray three-piece job, topped off with a stiff white collar that cut clear through his neck. He was wearing it now.

"John," he said, standing up and leaning over his desk to shake my hand. Cold as ever. But for the first time, he didn't tower over me. He was six feet, but I'd shot up past him in the past three years. It was a funny bit; old Epstein shaking my hand, while staring at my navel. Probably the first time in his life he'd ever had a patient taller than him. He readjusted his gaze.

"John," he repeated, clearly surprised, "you've grown. I remember the day you were born; barely four pounds."

"Yeah, well I don't remember that."

"Naturally. Your mother was afraid you wouldn't make it. But I told her preemies are a tough lot. Survivors."

I'd heard about the first few weeks of my life (spent in an incubator) more often than I'd cared to. My folks'd referred to me as a "skinny red chicken." I hoped Epstein wasn't going to dredge all that junk up again. Every time I outgrew shoes or my jeans inched up my legs, Mom would shake her head. "I don't understand it; you were such a *tiny* baby." It reminded me of a cartoon I'd seen once: Mr. Stork delivers a giant's baby to a normal mother by mistake. It made me feel freaky for a while. At night, I always thought I could *hear* myself growing.

"Sit down, John," he said, looking through my old medical file. Epstein had a protruding lower lip which he cultivated by constantly pulling on it. "It seems you're up to date on your shots. You don't need a tetanus booster; not until next year."

"I didn't come for a shot. I don't know why I'm here. Didn't you speak to my mother?"

"Yes I did. She was very upset. She'd like you to have a thorough checkup."

"But there's nothing wrong with me."

He smiled. "That's for the doctor to decide, isn't it? At the moment, your mother's concerned. She didn't give me many details on the phone, just that you've been acting strangely. Have you?"

"*I* don't think so."

"She said you're involved in some odd activities. You haven't gotten in with a bad group, have you, John?"

"Mom probably means Cliff, the ex-con. But I thought she didn't believe he existed."

"Do *you* believe he exists?"

"Of course I do."

Epstein nodded. "She also said you've been growing illegal drugs."

"I only had one lousy pot . . . I mean one *thing* of catnip. Which *she* flushed down the toilet. It's a misunderstanding, that's all."

"Aha," he said, as if listening to an idiot, "she told me you'd say that." Then he put on his serious take-two-aspirins expression. "Maybe you think this doesn't involve me, John, but I was touched by your mother's call. Naturally, I'm interested in all my patients and their growth. Oh, not just physical; everything. Children sometimes have a rough time of it, so you should be grateful your parents care. Your mother also mentioned some involvement with an older woman?"

For a guy who wasn't filled-in on the details, he was doing damn well!

"Aren't these questions for a psychiatrist?"

"Why? Do you think you need one?"

"No. Do you think you *are* one?"

He cleared his throat. "Let's begin the examination. Go in the other room and undress. I'll be in when you're ready."

When I left the room, I stripped to the waist, but that's all. I wasn't about to stick my behind on that cold, hard paper ever again.

Epstein came in, jabbed my finger, banged my knee, poked in my ears and stared down my throat. Then he checked my arms for puncture marks, supposedly looking for a good vein, but he didn't fool me. He probably wanted to know if I'd been mainlining catnip! After that, he made me wriggle my right foot, checking out my old fracture.

"Foot giving you any trouble?"

"No."

"Able to play football all right?"

"I don't play football."

"Basketball your game?"

"I hate sports."

"A big fellow like you?"

I hoped he wasn't about to give me that garbage the gym teacher dished out: Anyone over six feet owed it to the nation to become an athlete. Anyone over six feet four inches (for which I qualified by half an inch) was either a pervert or mentally disturbed if he didn't have his brains kicked out on some field or court.

Epstein jotted down my vital statistics in the typical doctor-chicken-scratch style. Then he gave me a patch test, poked and jabbed my stomach some more and took several vials of blood for God knows what reason.

"Okay, John, get dressed, and I'll see you back in my office."

As I stood up, he ripped the paper off the table and dumped it in the trash.

He was still scribbling when I returned to his office, looking more grimly professional than ever. "I find nothing wrong with you physically. Of course, we'll wait for the results of your blood tests, which'll take a few days. And naturally, some involvement in sports or hobbies might keep you more active and interested. Your mother mentioned writing?"

"That's not an interest. It's a dedication."

"Then you have no hobbies?"

"I collect roaches."

He stared solemnly. "Don't be defensive, John. Experimentation at your age is *normal*. After all, sex and drugs are part of our culture. Perhaps your mother's over-concerned. In any event, I'll speak to her when your tests come back."

Epstein stood up, indicating the visit was over, then made a perfunctory grab for the lollipop jar. Thinking better of it, with an embarrassed smile he said goodbye.

Instead of taking the bus to school, I walked cross-town, hoping to delay my arrival. Hoping, too, that Holloway had choked on another sandwich in the interim and had been carted off for emergency surgery. No such luck. I ran smack into him, heading for my math class.

"I spoke to your mother, Sandor. You're not allowed back in my class without a written apology."

"I know. I'll give it to you in the morning."

"Don't bother. Put it on the hall bulletin board. I want all my students to read it."

Typical!

The day kept going downhill. I was summoned to the principal's office, regarding my truancy. Then Beth Ann cornered me in science, to inform me my mother'd been at school that morning. According to Beth Ann, nothing short of *murder* could justify that.

"So what've you been doing, John?" she whispered. And why haven't you been doing it with me?"

"Don't bug me, Beth Ann, okay?"

"Holloway's really on your tail. You should've heard him this morning. I think he called you a subversive. I thought only Russians were subversive."

"Sorry I missed it. I was at the doctor."

"Nothing serious."

"Some blood tests and junk. My mother made me go. I don't want to talk about it, okay?"

"Sure, John, not another word."

What a laugh!

By three o'clock, a rumor had circulated the whole damn school. *I was involved in a paternity suit.*

Apparently, Beth Ann could conceive of nothing in a guy's life that didn't directly involve *sex.*

As I left school, I got dozens of high signs, sly smiles and jabs in the ribs.

"Thata boy, Johnno."

"Heard you've been keeping busy."

"Who would've guessed it!"

I couldn't wait to get out of the place.

I was actually glad to get home and start writing my apology to Holloway.

I decided to lay it on with a trowel:

It has come to my attention that I've been sadly lacking in the concrete, outward expressions of respect and admiration so rightly due an educator with your impressive credentials. Youthful exuberance and rebellion are my only feeble excuses for my shocking behavior. . . .

Yeah, I poured it on. It gave me no small measure of sadistic pleasure, writing something that would both satisfy Holloway and put him on at the same time. He totally lacked any recognizable sense of humor and was sure to believe every word of it. Meanwhile, the whole student body could have a laugh at his expense. I couldn't have *planned* it better.

Rapidly approaching page three of my tome, Mom came home.

"I left work early," she explained, dumping groceries on the kitchen counter. "I wanted to make sure you were behaving yourself."

"I am. I'm just finishing my letter to Holloway."

I stuck a notebook on top of the papers, but Mom was too sharp for that.

"Let me see it."

"It's just an apology, like I promised."

"Let me *see* it."

Mom read it and nodded knowingly. "If your teacher's stupid enough to consider this an apology, he is a nerd. If he's smart enough to know it's an insult, you'll be in double trouble, which you deserve. Now, for important business. What'd the doctor say?"

"He says I'm normal, no thanks to what *you* told him."

"I had to fill him in on the details."

"Well, they didn't impress him. In fact, he gave me the go-ahead for all the sex and drugs my heart desires."

"Janos!"

"I swear. He said experimentation's normal in young people."

"I can't believe it. Maybe there's something wrong with him, too."

Mom unpacked her groceries, practically hurling the cans in the closet. I'd only made the comment to prove what a mistake it had been, sending me to old Epstein. Now I realized, by putting it in those terms, I was actually *admitting* all the things I hadn't done.

"Relax," I said, trying to give her a ray of hope. "He has to get the tests back before he's *sure* I'm normal."

"What tests?"

"Blood tests—all kinds of junk. Epstein jabbed me all over with those icy hands. Why don't you knit him some gloves for Christmas?"

"Be quiet, Janos."

"The old guy's senile, too. He tried to give me a lollipop."

Mom grabbed a roll of paper towels and threw it across the room.

"Go to your room!" she shouted.

Parents!

I'd done everything Mom ordered, and she still wasn't satisfied!

Chapter 6

I would like people to leave my private life the hell alone. . . . E.H.

The next two days, Mom patiently awaited the results of my tests, firm in the belief that some microscopic corpuscle held the clue to my problems. Until all the evidence was in, she wouldn't be my judge. After all, there were many clinical possibilities. Perhaps the forceps delivery had affected my brain; or the extra oxygen I'd been given. Mom had begun thinking Dr. Epstein *might* be senile, but she knew the lab tests wouldn't lie.

Meanwhile, in school I had a period of grace. Apparently my asinine letter had satisfied Holloway. After I tacked it on the bulletin board, I heard not another word from him. The paternity suit rumor had calmed down, too. By now, most everyone realized it was ridiculous. I didn't know how to take that; maybe I should've been insulted.

I didn't have time to dwell on it. Mom was beginning to act *weird.* For one thing, she began leaving the butcher shop early so she'd be home when I returned from school. And she'd cleaned out the medicine cabinet, jettisoning all the old bottles of prescription drugs lurking behind the toothpaste. She even threw out the nosedrops!

Then I found a book on the refrigerator: *Understanding the Drug Culture.* Several passages were red-penciled.

Dad thought she might be overreacting, but Mom was adamant. "We've only one son, Joszef and he's not going down the toilet!"

The woman was flipping out, beyond talking to.

And it was freaking me out, too. I liked having the house to myself when I got home. Now, Mom's hot breath was constantly down my back. I couldn't think clearly enough to write. I kept envisioning her peeking through the keyhole or something. I was afraid to close my door, lest she think I was shooting up!

So I took my notebook up to the roof and wrote. It was real nice up there, surrounded by smokestacks and the steely-gray skyline. Occasionally, one of the epithets Mrs. Mancusso constantly hurled at Mr. Mancusso came wafting up through the courtyard and I'd jot it down. The rest of the time, I soaked up the E. B. White atmosphere, hoping for inspiration.

When I came down for dinner, both Mom and Dad stared at me with distrust and apprehension.

"The ax murderer hath returneth," I announced. "But not to worry. I've left my bloody chopper in the hall."

"Sit down and eat your soup," said Dad.

Oxtail, my least favorite thing. But lack of appetite would be another sign of abnormality, so I wedged them down my throat. Salty, lumpy jelly-balls: delicious.

I was midway through a swallow when the bell rang.

It was Clifford, and I was thrilled to see him. As he stood in the doorway, I realized he was the answer to all my youthful problems. Cliff was present when I'd bought the second-hand recorder. He could explain he'd given me the catnip plant. With a few words, he could clear up the entire mess. If only I'd had his address, this might have occurred to me sooner.

"I hope I ain't disturbin' nothin'," he said sheepishly.

"On the contrary," I said, greeting him with open arms and proudly escorting him into the kitchen to meet my folks. "Mom, Dad, this is Clifford, the ex-con I told you about. You don't mind my calling you that, do you, Clifford?"

"That's what I am, Johnny, an ex-con lug." He spit on his fingers to slick down his hair. "I wasn't expectin' ta meet your folks."

My folks put down their soup spoons and stared at each other, not knowing whether to stand or not.

Cliff's eyes darted furtively from one of them to the

75

other. "It's about our hobby," he whispered surreptitiously.

Poor Cliff. His childhood of clandestine gardening must've made him think it was a crime.

"It's okay, I've told my folks about you."

Relieved, he placed a paper bag on the table.

"I got ta thinkin' about whatcha said the other day, so I went to the joint. Couldn't stand it no longer, ya know. Those lugs wasn't takin' care of things. Made me so mad I went out and bought me some good stuff. I knew you'd want some."

Clifford ripped open the bag, proudly producing a giant bunch of poppies.

Mom and Dad couldn't have been more shocked if it'd been a bloody ax.

Of all the damn flowers in the damn world, why did Clifford have to bring me *poppies?* Poppies, from whence one produces *opium.* Mom's overnight crash course in drug abuse had taught her that much. Opium, far stronger than marijuana and much bigger trouble for me.

I didn't know what to say. Cliff grinned like a kid as he showed us the red flowers. Rapidly, Dad's face began matching their color.

"The best I ever got," said Cliff proudly. "I knew you'd want some."

Mom was so upset, she reverted to childhood, babbling in Hungarian.

Dad stood up, knocked over his soup bowl, then made a lunge for Clifford. Pushing the flowers from Cliff's hand, he shouted, "Get out of here, you criminal!"

For a second, as Cliff watched the flowers scatter to the ground, I thought he'd cry. Then instinct took over. He assumed his fighting stance, about to land Dad a left to the jaw. I quickly intervened, pulling him away. I dragged him from the kitchen, toward the front door, while Mom sputtered Hungarian curses. She was screaming and crying, too.

"Listen you guys," I shouted. "I'll straighten this all out later."

Dad came running from the kitchen, looking like Attila the Hun. Luckily, there were no tools of his trade lying around. If he'd had a cleaver, he would've split Cliff in two.

I pushed Cliff out the door, slammed it behind us, then hurried him down the back stairs. The poor guy was huffing and puffing when we got to the lobby. But we weren't safe yet. I dragged him up two blocks, until we got to a coffee shop.

"I need some milk," he said, dropping down into a booth. "My stomach's on the bum again."

I ordered two rounds of milk, then tried explaining. To my amazement, Clifford didn't require an explanation.

"Listen kid, I get it. Your folks think it's crazy . . . a big guy like you, foolin' around with flowers. I've been through it all my life. But I wished you woulda let me sock your old man one. It coulda straightened him out, ya know."

"That's not exactly it. You see . . ."

"Forget it, Johnny. See this mug? I got the broken nose, defendin' flowers. I know all about it."

It seemed simpler to let Cliff believe what his own life experience had proved to be true. Explaining what my parents really thought would only hurt his feelings. Besides, it sounded insane. That left *me* to straighten things out with my folks by myself. But I suspected Clifford had lost his credibility with them, anyway.

"I think it would be a good idea if you didn't come to the house again. Mom's been acting strange lately and . . ."

"Sure kid, no problem. I'll give ya my address at work. Anytime ya wanna talk, come over." He gulped down the remainder of his milk. "Gotta go now. If I'm late over at that place, the head man puts the thumb-screws ta me. But listen, Johnno, don't let it get ya down. Life's rough sometimes, but think how much crappier it'd be without flowers."

He slapped me on the back, then left. I watched him through the window as he shuffled down the street . . . a scarred-up lug Byron and Shelley would envy.

Now what?

I couldn't face going home until Dad had calmed down. I ordered a cheese sandwich, took out my notebook and chronicled the facts of the past few days. Maybe if they were written down in black and white, my folks would understand.

It all sounded utterly ridiculous, so I tore it up!

Then I walked around the neighborhood awhile, several hours, actually. I poked around Riverside Park, stared out at the boats on the Hudson and began feeling sorry for myself.

Why had I suddenly found myself embroiled in this maze of confusion? Why did my parents think I was an incurable goof-off, addict, lech and total waste of time?

Answer: because I wanted to *write.*

Nowhere in my detailed dissection of Hemingway's letters had I come across any indication that he'd had this problem. Rejections, yes; disappointments, sure; but no one thought he was *insane.*

After a clear analysis of the situation, I came to the conclusion it wasn't my problem at all . . . it was my parents'. For all they knew, they might have a *genius* lurking in their midst. Who knew what immortal masterpiece I might produce with a crumb of encouragement on their part? So what if I acted strange? They'd have to learn to live with it.

With firm resolve, I started home to tell them so. My resolve weakened a little when I discovered it was eleven o'clock. Still, I was determined to snare the lions in their den. Starting now, I'd see who I liked, write what I wanted, and interview whomever I pleased. And I'd continue to snoop on the Mancussos. Someday, when I'd immortalized them in literature, they'd be grateful.

Also, I'd never write another apology to a no-talent-nerd teacher, or subject myself to an examination by a senile old coot!

Going over these facts in my mind, I turned my key in the lock. The house was quiet. Damn, I hoped they hadn't gone to bed and stole my thunder.

I checked the living room. Mom and Dad were seated on the sofa, looking totally washed-out. Exhausted. In front of them was a giant ashtray filled with cigarette butts. They'd both quit smoking months before, but kept an emergency carton in the closet, in case life's tensions proved to be too much. Guess that'd happened, because the place was littered with stamped-out weeds. The room smelled like an old burnt shoe.

They both stared at me through a glassy-eyed daze.

Then Mom smiled, with an adoring glance, exclusively reserved for babies, cute, cuddly ones. "Janci." She sighed. "My dear, sweet Janci."

"We're glad you came back," said Dad, in a tone so respectful, I thought the Pope might be standing behind me. "Sit down, son, please."

"Listen, Dad, we've gotta talk."

"I know, son, I know. A long talk; that's what we all need."

Dad made a subservient gesture toward the easy chair, while Mom nodded and smiled wistfully.

Damn, they were acting weird. When I'd left a few hours before, I feared for my life. Now I was getting the royal treatment. Had they freaked out or what?

"Look," I explained, "I know I've been acting strange, but there's a simple explanation for everything. It has to do with my writing."

"We know, son," Dad nodded. "Now we know."

"I wish we'd known before," said Mom. "We could have *helped* you."

"Now, Anna, it isn't too late. It's never too late. True, special cases like Janos don't happen often."

"You were always such a quiet boy," said Mom, quivering close to tears. "Maybe that's why I never suspected. . . ."

As Dad leaned over to console her, I felt a cold sweat break out on my body. "Special cases," he'd said. *Special cases.* Suddenly, the whole horrible reality of the situation smacked me in the face.

The lab tests!

While I was out, they must've heard about the lab tests. Then there *was* something wrong with me. What was it? Leukemia, tuberculosis, heart trouble? How long did I have? Years, months, days, *what?*

All the books I never wrote or ever hoped to write seemed to float before my eyes. Dozens of leather-bound volumes, with little white wings, flying off into eternity. All those prizes and awards I'd never receive. All those spaces on the S shelf in libraries around the world. The foreign translations, the TV talk shows I'd never be on, the movie adaptations which couldn't be made . . . gone . . . all gone.

Was I getting carried away? Yeah, maybe I had some long, *lingering* illness, some rare disease that would dissipate my body slowly. A genetic imperfection, caused by prematurity. In that case, I might have years of literary productivity. Lots of famous authors struggled with illness yet managed to create classics. Robert Louis Stevenson had tuberculosis; Kafka, chronic poor health and depression. Still, they managed to create volumes that lived on after them.

Perhaps I could move to some tropical island and live out my remaining years. Or months. I'd go to Samoa, as Stevenson did. Or Tahiti, maybe. The sun could bake down on my frail, withered body by day, and I'd write by night. When I grew too weak to hold a pen, I'd dictate into my tape recorder. Thank goodness I already had a tape recorder.

No, I was being too pessimistic. Maybe I didn't have a fatal disease at all; merely an incurable one; something that would make people shun me on sight. Could it be acromegaly, where the head and feet grow huge? Maybe that's why I never stopped growing. Or did I have neuro-fibrosis, like the Elephant Man? Damn, I'd have to wear a bag on my head.

All these thoughts and more bombarded my mind in a matter of moments. But I was being selfish. Glancing at my parents, I knew they must be suffering, too. My bravery might help us all get through this. But first, I'd have to know the facts.

"It's all right," I said, "tell me everything. When did you find out?"

"Right after you left," said Dad.

"Well, what is it? What's it called? What've I got?"

Mom smiled weakly. "Genius, Janci. There's no other word for it."

Poor Mom was so upset, she must've been mixing up her languages again. Or maybe she meant "genus" something: referring to whatever species of germ was presently attacking my vital organs.

I was afraid to ask, but I did.

"How long have I got?"

Dad smiled. (Which I thought extremely inappropriate, not to mention insensitive.) "It's not something that comes and goes, son. When you've got it, it lasts forever."

Forever . . . a relative term, under the circumstances.

"But," he added, "I don't think you got it from me. Maybe from you, Anna?"

Mom looked *flattered*. "No, Joszef, no one in my family ever had it. But your Uncle Zoltan played the violin."

Their conversation was eluding me. "What the heck is this disease, anyway? Exactly how sick am I?"

"Don't talk like that, Janci," said Mom. "I know you think we've misunderstood you, and we have. Maybe *all* geniuses are misunderstood. I suppose talent can be a terrible thing, sometimes."

"Wait a minute," I said. "I'm not *dying?*"

Dad looked hurt. "Have we made you feel so stifled? Well, it's your fault, too. If you'd shown us some of your writing, we would've known."

"But we're not excusing the drugs," Mom interrupted. "We know what drove you to it; but even if you are a genius, you have to quit. Thank goodness I didn't find any more plants in your room, only your wonderful writing."

Mom gestured toward the table. Under the ashtray filled with cigarette butts rested a pile of my typewritten pages.

Finally, I realized what was going on. After I left, my folks must have snooped in my room, found my writing folder and read it. And liked it, loved it, thought I was a genius, even though what they saw were only rough, undigested sketches, so to speak.

Recognition at last, while I was still in my youth; who would've believed it. Bless their dear sweet immigrant hearts. I immediately excused their invading my privacy. Their thoughtful, intelligent criticism of my work totally vindicated them.

To think I'd hidden my work, afraid they'd consider it silly and stupid. Now I wanted to share each line and bask in the glory of their admiration. How I'd misjudged Mom. She *did* have faith in me. When I dropped dead, she too, would carry my book around to publishers until I received my posthumous Pulitzer. But I wasn't going to die, was I? I was twice blessed: a genius, and alive as well!

"You really loved it, eh? Which bit did you like best?"

"All of it, Janos, every word," said Dad, patting the

pages in front of him. "Shocking, but good, solid writing. How'd you come up with the idea?"

"It's all true, Dad, every word. I considered changing some facts, but I've told it like it is."

He seemed concerned. "It can't be true. No one in our family has ever . . . besides, the doctor checked you out. Nothing wrong. Nothing at all. He called today."

"Don't tease us, Janci," smiled Mom. "You've never been to war. And you've only seen pictures of Paris and Spain. How did you know so much about bullfights? From all those books in your room, I suppose."

Paris? Bullfights? My heart sank. They weren't talking about *my* writing. Mom and Dad had discovered *Ernest Hemingway. He* was the genius they referred to. Hell, everyone knew that, but what about *me?*

"Is that all you liked? What about the other stuff? My notes on Clifford and all those pages on the Mancussos and the Onion Bag Man."

Mom shook her head. "Why waste your time with silly stuff when you have such a talent?"

So. They *did* think my work silly and stupid. Too bad I didn't have a fatal disease. It was better than dying of embarrassment.

Hell, what'd they know? How stupid can you be, not to recognize Hemingway? Every school kid should know that book. Eight years of high school between them, and they'd probably never heard his name. So who cared? Their literary criticism was worthless!

"I didn't write that book."

Mom smiled. "Don't be silly, Janci. It's all here, typed out."

"Sure, I *typed* it. But I didn't *write* it."

"I don't understand," said Dad. "What's the difference?"

"It's *already* a book, Dad. Written years ago, by Ernest Hemingway."

"Who?"

His denseness infuriated me. *"Hemingway,* one of America's most famous novelists. He won the Nobel Prize."

Mom looked down at the pages, as if some treasure had just been ripped from her grasp. "You mean it's not yours? You *stole* it from someone?"

"I didn't steal it, I typed it. Writers do that sometimes. Damn, I don't expect you to understand. Hemingway wasn't understood, either. When that book came out, lots of people thought it was garbage. Know why? Because some stupid critic on his hometown paper said so. And her name was Fanny *Butcher!"*

The fateful irony of that remark totally escaped my folks. Mom was still trying to grasp the incomprehensible deed of retyping.

"So it's already been written, Janci? Why write a book that's already been written?"

"Inspiration," I shouted. "But you wouldn't know about that."

"Hold it," said Dad. "You mean for the past few

months all you've been doing in that room is adding to the roach pile and *typing?*"

"And slaving over research you and Mom consider garbage!"

With my voice approaching a dangerous falsetto, I realized the utter uselessness of continuing the conversation.

"Oh, what's the use. All butchers are alike!"

I threw my jacket back on, then slammed out of the apartment.

Chapter 7

_____

. . . That terrible mood of depression of whether it's any good or not is what is known as The Artist's Reward. . . . E.H.

The dark streets mirrored my total desolation. No artist is totally appreciated in his lifetime, but he shouldn't be considered an idiot, either!

"Papa" Hemingway had all Europe to wander when he wanted to clear his head. I only had Broadway. Broadway, filled with nameless faces on their way to nowhere.

I needed to see Cliff, someone who could empathize with being misunderstood and rejected. I had the address where he worked in my pocket, only a few blocks away. Probably an all-night greasy spoon.

It turned out to be an all-night bar and grill. Gilhooley's was one of the truly ethnic Irish joints left in the neighborhood. It was heavy with the smell of whiskey, mingling with corned beef and cabbage: a place where someone's always being hurled through the swinging bar doors out into the street. It was a typical night, judging from the police car parked outside with lights flashing.

"Is Clifford around?" I asked, making my way to the bar.

Two red-nosed guys, typical barflies, seemed permanently glued to their seats. They didn't hear me.

"I'd like to talk to Cliff."

The bartender wiped a filthy rag across the counter. "You mean Karlbach? He's in the kitchen, but not for long."

"Can I see him?"

"Sure. You his parole officer?"

"Just a friend."

"Who're you kiddin', mister? That bum don't have a friend. And he don't have a job no more, neither."

"What happened?"

"He hauled off and socked one of the customers. Broke his nose, ribs, too, maybe. Blood all over the floor. Those ex-cons never learn. Give 'em a break and they blow it."

"Which way's the kitchen?"

He gestured to the door behind the bar. As I pushed it open, I saw two cops standing beside Clifford. He was leaning over the sink, blood pouring from his face onto the sudsy stack of dishes.

"Hey, Johnno," he said, grabbing a towel and slapping it on his face. "Good ta see ya."

"What's been going on?"

"Nothin', no big deal."

One cop slipped a pad from his back pocket. "Big enough. It'll land you back in jail." He looked at me. "You his parole officer?"

"Just a friend. Can I talk to him?"

"We're taking him down to the station for booking. When that guy he assaulted gets out of Emergency, he's coming down to swear out a warrant."

"I just want to speak to him a minute."

The cops looked at each other. "Okay, we'll get some coffee at the bar. But make it quick."

Cliff grabbed his pinstripe from a hook and put it on. "Nice of ya to visit, kid." The fight had opened up the scar above his eye, making his face look like hamburger. "Grab that stool and sit down."

"Why'd you get in a fight, Cliff?"

"My nature, I guess."

"But you've broken your parole, not to mention someone's bones. That means you're going back to prison."

"That's life, I guess."

I didn't get it. Cliff hardly seemed upset, but I sure was. What good could he do me behind bars? How could I continue my research, finish my tape recordings?

Our two talks had only scratched the surface. To create a full-bodied character, I needed much more background material.

"Cliff, why'd you do such a stupid thing? Did you have to blow your top like that?"

"Listen kid, that guy asked for it. He comes roarin' in here, blind drunk, tellin' me his glass ain't clean. So I told 'em where to shove it." Reliving the incident, his face beamed with pride. "He got the worsta the deal. They hada *carry* 'im out."

"But you can't go back to prison. Not *now*."

He shrugged. "Look around ya, Johnny."

I glanced at the dirty walls, the grease-covered stove, the flypaper ceiling and the stacks of filthy dishes.

"What d'ya think *this* is?" he asked, philosophically. "And ya should see the room I got in that flea-bag down the street. Ain't no space for a bed, My cell in the joint's bigger. Na, kid, this ain't freedom. The system's got a way of screwing up lugs like me. It makes us go round and round till we get back where we started. Hell, I tried. I even brung in flowers for the bar, but some drunken slob threw up on 'em. Na, it won't work. At least in prison, I got my garden. What've I got here? Nothin'. Except you, Johnny. I'll miss the talks about flowers."

"Yes, our talks, Cliff, they have to continue. There's lots more I want to know."

He seemed touched. "Guess I disappointed ya, huh? Hell, I ain't no good with people, never have been. They don't make no sense. So let's face it, a guy like me's got three strikes against 'im from the start. You oughta write me off."

Write him off: prophetic words. With Cliff back in prison, I'd have to write off my *book,* at least until he got out again.

"How long will they give you this time?"

"Who knows? Two years, maybe three. I'm what they call a repeat offender. With any luck, they'll throw the book at me."

Cliff's literary references were sadly ironic. "You mean you *want* to go back to prison?"

"Can't say I mind. The lugs inside ain't no worse'n the lugs out here. And I miss my garden. Ain't had my hands in one decent plot o' dirt since I left!"

So that was it! Cliff had engineered the whole thing. For him, prison was a revolving door through which he'd constantly reenter. Even with time off for good behavior, he'd only bop somebody else to be near his flowers again. That meant I'd *never* finish my research.

I felt awful. With Cliff in the pokey, I saw my main character slipping through my fingers and nothing I could do to stop it.

"Hey, don't take it so bad, kid. The cards were stacked against me. But I'll write ya, okay? I ain't good with words, so don't expect much."

The two policemen returned. "Okay, Karlbach, let's get moving."

One took his handcuffs and clamped them on Cliff's

wrists. He didn't blink. In fact, he look relieved; like some lost kid who'd just been found by the cops.

"Hope I'm back in the joint in time ta see my roses."

"Oh, you'll be back all right," said the officer. "This time, they'll throw the book at you!"

Cliff threw me a knowing smile as I followed them to the patrol car.

"Keep your nose clean, Johnno," he shouted, then waved as the policemen drove him off.

Staring at the car's flashing lights until they were tiny pinpoints in the darkness, I felt all hope of completing my book disappearing with them. My magnum opus, my testament to the endurance of the human spirit, had been cruelly ripped from my typewriter and imprisoned behind bars, too.

Or was it a lost cause? Maybe I could find a new main character and chuck all the ideas with Clifford. Sure, some clever changes and alterations . . . "Yet a hundred visions and revisions" . . . and I could write him out altogether.

Who was I kidding? Karlbach was the inspiration I'd waited for. Without him, all my folders filled with research were nothing but background material. He was the glue that held it all together: the pulsing beat that gave it heart. Without him, it was nothing, and I knew it. Meeting up with Cliff had taken me down a new literary road, which had now led to a dead end. How ironic that I'd thought of him as a Dead End Kid when I first met him. How horribly prophetic, too.

Knowing my work-in-progress would progress no more, I turned down to Riverside Park, to walk home along the Drive. The day had seemed a thousand hours long, yet I couldn't end it.

I racked my brain for a line from Hemingway's letters to bring me consolation, but found none. I seemed abandoned. My parents had already discounted my literary efforts as silly and unimportant. They'd probably be thrilled to learn Cliff was back in prison, putting an end to a "disagreeable chapter" in their son's life.

I carried the heavy burden of knowing that not a soul understood or cared.

My head still in a fog, I climbed the stone stairs to the Fireman's Monument and sat on a bench at the base of the marble statue. Through the darkness, I could see a girl slouched on the bench opposite.

"Hi, John," she said, coming closer.

It was Beth Ann.

"Isn't it late to be out here?" I asked, annoyed my brooding had been interrupted.

"Guess so."

"Why don't you go home?"

"Mom's got a guy upstairs, as usual. It's a small apartment, not big enough for three of us."

"Oh."

She took a cigarette from her pocket. "Want one?"

"No, I don't smoke those things."

"It's not pot, silly; just a regular weed."

"I don't smoke those, either."

"Wish I didn't." She sighed. "But I'm hooked. Listen, I'm sorry that rumor got started in school."

"Forget it."

"I didn't do it, honest. I just told some of the kids you'd had a blood test. But I might have started it myself, if I'd thought it would make you notice me."

"It doesn't matter," I said blankly. "Nothing matters any more."

"I've felt like that, too, lots of times. Wanna talk about it?"

"Hardly."

Beth Ann moved closer, and I got a whiff of her perfume. *"Do* you notice me, John? I mean, do you think I'm pretty?"

Through the darkness, I couldn't make out whatever garish outfit Beth Ann must be wearing. I couldn't see the ton of makeup on her face or the crazy color of her hair. Underneath it all, *was* she actually pretty? Who knew? Who cared?

"Sure, Beth Ann, you're real pretty."

"Do you mean it? Never mind, I'll pretend you do. I pretend you notice me sometimes, too, but I know you don't really pay attention."

Attention. Damn, I wanted more than that; I wanted *admiration*. I could've had it, too, if Cliff hadn't thrown a monkey wrench in things.

"I bet you could get any girl you want, John, a talented guy like you."

Talented, sure. What good did it do me? My writing

efforts would be consigned to my desk, the unheralded, unwritten, masterpiece of my youth.

"Maybe you'll let me read some of your stuff sometime? I'd like to read it, even though I don't know much about writing."

Who did? Certainly not my parents. They knew *nothing*. Hell, maybe it'd be better to give the book a decent burial, rather than let it lie naked before people unable to fathom its depths.

"What do you think? Would you?"

"What?"

"Let me read your writing."

"No," I said. "No one will ever see it. And it'll never be completed."

"What do you mean?"

"I mean it's over, finished. All that's left is a decent burial!"

Even through the darkness, I could see the surprised look on her face.

"Good night, Beth Ann, I've gotta go now."

"Wait a minute," she called after me.

I didn't look back.

My parents were still up when I got home. They hadn't moved from their spot on the sofa; only now, the cigarette pile was twice as large.

"Why'd you run out like that, son? We've got things to settle."

"It's all settled, Dad. In fact, it's over."

"Don't be dramatic, Janci. While you were gone, your dad and I figured out your problem. You have no responsibilities. That's why you run around with criminals and grow drugs."

"Work's what you need," Dad agreed. Respectable, hard work."

"So," Mom continued, "starting tomorrow, you begin work in the store. Every day after school, all day Saturday."

So that was their Master Plan. I was going to be a butcher, like my father and my father's father. I knew the old saying, "When God closes one door, he opens another," but I hadn't figured the new path planned for me would lead to Dad's butcher shop.

Hell, what did it matter? If I couldn't write my book, I didn't care what I ultimately did. Butchery would suffice.

"Fine, Dad. It sounds like a swell idea."

Chapter 8

. . . Writing is the loneliest of all trades. . . . E.H.

Casting off the trappings of what I'd hoped would be a year-long project wasn't easy; but necessary. I couldn't live in a room with books and articles, piles of research material I'd accumulated. They were haunting specters, memories of unfulfilled dreams. So I stayed home from school and did what had to be done.

I began by returning all my overdues to the library. The bill was staggering. Dad advanced me the money, with the understanding I'd pay it back from my salary. By my calculations, I'd be working for the library for a month!

Next, I set about clearing everything from my room.

The magazines and newspapers, I dumped in the incinerator. I retrieved a year's dirty laundry from the drawers and closet. I stacked up tons of paperbacks and stored them in the basement, after which, I tackled the bug problem.

I bought a bomb that activates like a hand grenade, let 'er rip, then slammed the door. When I returned, every insect was totalled: heaps and piles of tiny brown bodies in every corner. If there was an Archy among them, he didn't survive. It was a cruel lesson for a potentially gifted roach: society has no time for genius.

Mom's obvious delight at the new state of my room was coupled by an equally obvious concern for my state of mind.

"Janci, don't get rid of *everything*. Why bury your typewriter in the closet?"

"I won't be using it for a while."

She shook her head. "Why must you always go to extremes?"

How could I explain? Would Dickens have written *A Christmas Carol*, without including Scrooge? What was *Gone with the Wind*, without Rhett Butler? *A Study in Scarlet*, without Sherlock Holmes? *Catcher in The Rye*, without Holden Caulfield, for heaven sake? . . . fragmented, senseless *words . . . meaningless*.

With appropriate reverence, I placed all my notes and research material in a cardboard box. On top, I put the fifty-two pages I'd written after I met Cliff, the beginning of my great work. I couldn't resist reading some of it just one more time, before it was cruelly consigned to its tomb.

The story opens with Cliff wandering through the Salvation Army, his first day out of stir. (I included some bitingly witty dialogue between him and Murphy.) This gets interrupted when the Onion Bag Man wanders in to grub a quarter, whereupon Cliff explains he's spent his last dime on marigold seeds. Of course, this comment intrigues the two men, and they ask how he came to be interested in flowers. This scene is cleverly followed by a flashback to Clifford's youth, scrounging around Hell's Kitchen.

Suddenly, I became too depressed to continue reading. The untimely death of my main character was a bitter pill to swallow. With a heavy heart, I placed my opus-interruptus on the darkened top shelf of the closet, sighed and slammed the door.

Then I surveyed my room. It was barren and orderly, reflecting no personality at all. The only spark of life came from one shelf of books I'd decided to keep: my favorite novels, the ones I read for pleasure, not reference. Naturally, Hemingway's letters were there, too.

Okay, circumstances had forced me off the literary path temporarily.

But I'd return someday!

At three thirty the next day, all my noble resolve instantly vanished when I set foot inside Dad's store.

I truly hated the place . . . the smells of raw meat,

the tools of mutilation proudly displayed behind the counter . . . even the smell of sawdust turned my stomach.

Actually, the front of the store wasn't too bad: plump yellow chickens resting in trays. As an artistic addition, Mom had sprinkled beds of parsley around them. The cold cuts counter looked okay, too. I had no moral objection to giant hunks of liverwurst or bologna. They were byproducts, far removed from their original source.

But I was in for a shock when Dad gave me a tour of the freezer room in back. There's a good reason butchers don't let customers see what goes on in there!

Whenever a customer orders a special cut, Dad disappears from view behind the door. Moments later, he returns with some edible slab of something. *But* . . . if the customers knew from whence that product emanated, they'd *all* become vegetarians!

Needless to say, the freezer room was cold as hell. If it hadn't been, it'd still send chills down my spine. The damn place was an animal morgue where pigs and cows reposed; only they weren't awaiting a decent burial, but further mutilation. The scene evoked Goya's etchings, depicting the horrors of war: dozens of carcasses hanging from hooks, split down the middle. Hoofs, feet and tails swung in front of my face. Pig's heads, eyes staring blankly into space, awaited their fate in a cold jellied mass of headcheese.

"All choice cuts," said Dad proudly.

"Not the animal's choice, I bet."

"Listen Janos, there's lots to learn," he said, slapping a steer's haunches. With proprietary pleasure, he slid his hand down the side of the carcass, like a professor giving an anatomy lesson. "The shoulder's where you get your chuck, rib steaks from the rib, of course, and short steaks from the loin. And here's the flank, the rump and the shank."

"Can't I just sell bologna?"

Dad, seeing my face turning green, decided to resume the lesson later. Leaving the Crypt of Horror, he slammed the door behind us. I was actually happy to get behind the counter, where no bovine eyes could mock me.

My first sale of the afternoon didn't go *too* badly. An old man wanted a pound of sliced ham, so Dad showed me how to work the slicer. *Four times.* I just couldn't get the hang of it. Either the pieces came out razor thin or in unchewable hunks. And I couldn't figure out where to put my fingers without getting them chopped off. It made me wonder how many unsuspecting customers were actually eating slivered-butcher-finger embedded in their sandwiches! I finally managed to make the slices uniform, then threw in the unchewable hunk for free. The old guy was overjoyed at this magnanimous gift and left the store happy.

Next, someone wanted a two-pound flank steak, so Dad gestured me in the right direction. I took a red slab of meat from the case and threw it on the scale. Two pounds, exactly.

"Trim it, please," said the woman.

"Okay, lady," I said, dumping a mess of parsley on top.

She stared at me as if I were defective. "Mr. Sandor," she hissed, glancing at Dad. "Please have this person trim my steak."

"Of course, Mrs. Beasley."

Dad took the steak from the scale and cut off the excess fat. "We always trim twice, Janos. Once in the back room, then once for the customer. It gives them confidence in the meat."

Slowly, I began learning the psychological import of such menial chores. And I began seeing Dad in a new light. He really loved his work; *revere* wouldn't be too strong a word. He also knew all his customers' names and talked with them.

"How's your little girl, Mrs. Ramsey? Still have the flu? Maybe some chicken soup. I've got a chicken, soft as butter."

Yeah, for Dad, boning-out was a fine art, approached with surgeon's skill. For him, the back room didn't represent X number of slaughtered animals. It meant a succulent steak for Mr. Coogan after work, a lovely chicken liver salad for Mrs. Henroth's cocktail party and a soft hamburger patty for toothless Mr. Simpson. If there was such a thing, Dad was a humanitarian butcher.

But that didn't help *me* much. I was still too queasy to stand by the counter where visible body parts resided, because *I* was a humanitarian, too. The pig's feet reminded me of some poor porky, limping through life. In fact, *all* the meat had faces . . . some, fondly remembered friends from childhood literature: Bambi, Goosey Gander, Wilbur Pig, Chicken Little. The massive tongue, from some cow "untimely ripped" rested beside the brain, awaiting Dr. Frankenstein's scalpel.

"You're doing good, Janci," said Mom, patting my shoulder. "Wasn't I right? Work takes your mind off crazy things. Someday maybe you'll even cut a piece of meat right the first time."

And so it went. Each day after school, I worked in the store, all day Saturday. After two weeks, the simple uncreative life actually took my mind off my creative loss. Or else, I was too tired to think about it. The world of letters seemed far removed from cow innards and knockwurst.

Then, I received a note from Cliff. It came from Downstate Prison in Fishkill, New York.

Hi, kid . . .
    Pleaded guilty and got back here fast.
    Missed my daffodils, but I'll see the
    roses. They're gonna be big bruisers
    this year.
    Come see me if ya can.
               Clifford Karlbach

Fishkill was only about a hundred miles away. I could hop on a bus and go up there some weekend. I'd bring my tape recorder and tons of paper. Hallelujah! My book wasn't a lost cause, after all; it had been reprieved.

I'd have to cool it, though: keep playing straight with my folks for a while. We were finally on an even keel, and I didn't want to blow it by "renewing bad relationships."

Besides, I had a new relationship I was trying to deal with at the moment . . . with Beth Ann. Not a relationship exactly, but she was after me, for sure. My first day on the job, she popped up by the cold-cut counter. She acted real surprised to see me, but that was a lie. I'd noticed her staring at me through the window!

"My mom always shops at Grumbley's, down the street," she explained, "but I don't like his hamburger."

"Grumbley's?" Dad snorted. "No wonder. He puts fat in his ground round."

The minute Dad thought he had a potential "convert," he ordered me to be extra attentive to Beth Ann; encouragement she hardly needed.

"What'll it be?" I asked.

"A pound of ham," she said, catching her reflection in the case. "Like my new lipstick, John?"

Butchery was a big enough problem, without dealing with a femme fatale.

"No I don't," I said bluntly. "It looks like calves' blood. You'd look better without it."

I thought that would put an end to things, but it was only the beginning. Each afternoon she came in the shop, ordering a pound of this, half a pound of that. And always wearing some new kind of face glop with which to tempt me. I told her they were all awful. By the end of the week, she gave up and came in with no makeup at all. That's when I realized she *was* pretty, very. She'd also washed the crazy vegetable dye from her hair, revealing a nice, normal shade of blonde.

Dad was confused. "Is that the same girl who . . . no, it couldn't be."

"But it is."

Dad took personal credit for Beth Ann's improved appearance, certain it was the superior cuts of meat she'd been eating!

In a funny way, I didn't mind her come-ons. I may have even looked forward to her stopping by each day. Hell, it meant a few minutes away from the headcheese and bloodwurst.

We'd talk about all sorts of things: school, teachers we hated, even clothes. I told her I didn't like flashy dressers, and she got the point. After a while, her outfits began to calm down, too. When things got busy in the store, she'd buy something she probably didn't need or want, then go. Anyway, our conversations began making me feel less of an outcast.

Which I definitely was feeling. Lately, kids around school were giving me sly looks or the cold shoulder. Was it an aftermath of that paternity rumor garbage? Or was I getting paranoid?

Well, I wasn't imagining one thing: I was definitely

a missing person in Holloway's class. Since I'd handed in my apology, he acted like I didn't exist. He never called my name, and all my assignments were handed back without a grade. Obviously a deliberate strategy on his part, but I was getting ticked.

I decided to confront him, so I stopped him in the hall one afternoon, after class.

"Why haven't you been grading my papers?"

"Oh, you noticed."

I found his sideburns ridiculous, his smiling air of superiority annoying and his suede elbow patches an academic affectation.

"I thought you'd prefer grading your own papers, Sandor," he said (obviously, relishing the confrontation), "since you think you know more about teaching than I do."

I couldn't help but look surprised.

"It's true, isn't it? You're not impressed with my class."

An understatement!

"Well, I'm very impressed with you, Sandor; at least I *was*. You're the classic talented student a teacher hopes to guide. And impress, as well. Oh yes, I have an ego, too; but not as inflated as yours. Did you think I bought that apology on the bulletin board? I left it there as a *put-on,* because I'd written you off. I know I have no hope of reaching you, but I have twenty-nine other students in your class who need attention."

As he leaned against the radiator, I realized I'd conveniently given him the opportunity he'd been waiting for: a lecture.

"Know your problem, John? Oh, you're creative, sure; but you're unaware anyone else exists. You thought that pencil essay ridiculous, so you discounted it for *everyone*. But there are kids without your talent; some who've never grasped an abstract concept. That exercise was for *them*. It helped some of them a lot."

Dirty pool, real below-the-belt stuff. Mocking me and using my talent as a weapon. Obviously, Holloway was covering up his own shortcomings by projecting them on me.

"I still want my work recognized," I insisted. (It may have sounded pouty.) "That's your job, isn't it?"

"Part of it. A more important part is recognizing individual potential. Yours is impressive, but nothing you've done in my class merits more than a C."

Now I had him! Even before the phoney apology I'd written two damn good stories, Holloway hadn't graded, either. He merely put a notation on top: SEE ME. Naturally, I didn't.

"How about my City Streets essay?"

"Derivative."

"And my story about the welfare family?"

"Pretentious and embarrassing."

Who was he kidding? I bet he'd never *read* it. I refreshed his feeble memory. "It was called Struggle for Survival."

"Yes, I remember . . . eight starving immigrants, huddled around a stove. Modeled after Pearl Buck, no doubt; but without her heart."

Hot anger burned my cheeks. What was he talking about . . . ego? I'd accepted the fact that my book had had to be interrupted . . . that I wasn't a genius, not yet. What did he mean . . . pretentious? Because I set high goals? At least *I* set the standards. Holloway was telling me my work was *mediocre,* not my magnum opus, but some trivial class assignment. What nerve. What unadulterated gall!

"I still want my papers graded," I shouted. "It's your job, so do it!"

"All right, Sandor," he said (making it sound more like a threat than an agreement), "hand in this week's assignment, and I'll grade it."

Okay. I hadn't looked at the worksheet yet, but I'd produce something brilliant and make him eat his words!

That afternoon, while hacking away at chicken parts, I thought of Holloway, each thrust of the cleaver aimed at him. Damn, I would have loved to stew his giblets! How dare he take that patronizing tone with me. Me, who by his own admission was the most talented student he'd ever had, or hoped to. How dare he use my put-on against me. Had he? I wondered. Were kids laughing at me, not him? Was that why I was getting sly glances and cold shoulders? That'd be too much to endure!

Pearl Buck without heart, eh? If I had Holloway's

heart, I'd display it in the meat case. But a small dried-up-prune heart like that wouldn't make decent dog meat!

"Janos," shouted Dad, "what're you doing with my chicken?"

I looked down at the butcher block. I'd pulverized the thing! Too bad it wasn't dessicated-Holloway-pate.

"Janci," said Mom, as I let the cleaver descend again, "maybe you should go home early? I think you're working too hard."

I glanced at myself in the case. A crazy, maniacal nut stared back. "I guess you're right," I agreed. "I'm feeling lousy."

Walking along Broadway, Holloway's comments banged on my brain. *Derivative. Pretentious.* Cold, calculated criticism.

Hell, I could be cold and objective, too; so I decided to judge my work myself.

When I got home, I rummaged through my now neat and orderly desk. All the year's English assignments were in the bottom drawer. I took out Struggle for Survival, which I remembered was a gem. Maybe not Pearl Buck, but a pearl, anyhow.

Before writing it, I'd watched the local nightly news for a week. During the winter, they've always got stories on families setting their places on fire or freezing to death from lack of heat. Great background material.

My characters were Manuel, Maria and their six starving children. The stove in their one-room tenement was their only protection from the cold. Each evening, they'd cook their meager meal of beans on it, then keep it ablaze through the night for warmth. The story ended with everyone burning to death when the plastic statue of Our Lady, kept above the stove caught fire.

In my unemotional opinion, it had everything: tenderness, tragedy and lots of background material. I didn't get it. What *more* could Holloway want?

Whatever he wanted, he'd get it in the next assignment. Like a raging bull, I ran to the closet and retrieved my typewriter from its short sleep. I took out my English paper, to check that week's assignment. Lesson Plan: write a two page essay entitled, My Friend.

I couldn't believe it. What a pedestrian, secondgrade assignment. How could I be inspired by such mundane material?

I pushed the typewriter away in disgust and came to a final, ultimate irrevocable conclusion.

Holloway was an ass!

Chapter 9

─ ─ ─ ─ ─ ─ ─ ─ ─ ─

. . . A writer has to make up stories for them to be rounded and not flat like photographs. But he makes them up out of what he knows. . . . E.H.

Hell hath no fury like a writer scorned!

I had no appetite for dinner that night, even though it was my favorite: spaghetti. I poked at the pasta a while, then pushed the plate away.

Around seven o'clock, the bell rang, and Dad answered.

"It's that nice girl," he said. "The one who always comes in the store."

"Beth Ann? What's she doing here?"

Mom smiled coyly. "Go see, Janci."

(I suspected she might've been doing some match-making behind my back.)

"Am I interrupting something?" asked Beth Ann, leaning in the doorway. She was minus her five-inch heels —which made her look four feet tall next to me.

"No, dinner's over. What's up?"

"I'd like to talk to you. Could we go for a walk, maybe?"

Yeah, I needed some air to clear my head of thoughts of Holloway.

"Sure. Wanna go down to the monument?"

"No, not there. Some kids are hanging out there; you know the scene. Let's walk in the park, okay?"

As I grabbed my jacket, Dad passed by.

"How was that flank steak?"

"Delicious, Mr. Sandor, just like you promised."

Dad smiled contentedly, then patted my back. "Have a nice time, you two."

(Yep. I was definitely the object of a small conspiracy.)

Beth Ann and I walked through the park, but she didn't say much. I could tell something was on her mind, though, because she didn't bat her eyes or ask about makeup. Minus the glop and heels, she looked much younger, and definitely cute. The little freckle patches on her nose were decidedly appealing.

"Wanna stop in the playground?" she asked.

"Sure."

We sat on a bench, watching the few toddlers remaining in the sandbox making giant heaps and peaks of sand. Once they'd built them, they rammed them through with metal cars.

Beth Ann smiled at them, then offered me a stick of gum.

"What, no butts?"

"Trying to quit. You weren't in the store today. I asked your mom why and she said you didn't feel good; acting funny. Is something wrong?"

"Only the cruel injustices of life, that's all."

She nodded. "Your folks are real nice, John. They always talk to me when I come in. And your dad smiles at everyone."

"I'd no idea you were all such chums."

"Well, I think they like me, too. I hope so." Beth Ann stared at me, as if trying to find words to say something important. "How's your book coming along?"

"It isn't."

"You're not writing any more?"

"Nope. I've got fifty-two pages, wrapped in mothballs."

"Wanna talk about it?"

"There's nothing to say."

"There's always something to say," she argued, kicking the dirt with her feet. "People shouldn't ever keep stuff inside; it's not good. That's one of the things I learned in this group I belong to."

I had to laugh. "That spaced-out bunch? They're so

high, none of them know what they're saying half the time."

She didn't understand. "Oh, you mean the kids at the monument? No, I don't pal around with them anymore; well, hardly ever. Even when I did, I didn't. I mean, I only smoked *cigarettes*. I've never told them that, though. Sure, sometimes I hang out there when Mom has a hot date. It beats sitting in the laundry room. But I know they're a bunch of jerks and wipe-outs. Not like you, John. You want to *do* something with your life, not throw it away. That's right, isn't it?"

"Sure, but what are you driving at?"

"I think you know. It's something you told me that night at the monument. It's been on my mind, and I wondered if you meant it."

I tried remembering what I might've said that night. Cliff being hauled off to prison had shaken me up. Oh yeah, I'd told Beth Ann she was pretty (before I'd actually realized she was). Guess the girl needed *lots* of convincing.

"Sure, Beth Ann, I meant every word."

Instead of looking pleased, she seemed upset. "That's what I figured, but I wanted to be sure. You know, John, sometimes people make mistakes . . . do crazy things . . . mainly because they think nobody cares."

"Yeah, I know how *that* feels," I agreed. (I still hadn't shaken the enticing thought of Holloway-giblets.)

"This group I belong to has helped *me,*" she said.

"We meet once a week at the hospital. Messed-up kids, mainly. Some are just thinking about it, but lots have tried it; two and three times, even."

"Tried what?"

She seemed annoyed. "You're not gonna help me at all, are you, John? Okay, I'm not afraid of the word; not anymore. Suicide."

"*Suicide?* You mean *you've* . . ."

"Yeah, last year. Don't you remember? I was out of school for a month."

I didn't.

"Yeah, I'd had it with my mom and all her boyfriends. Guess I was trying to get a rise out of her. But I used a rusty razor blade and botched things." She smiled weakly. "Mom had a fit when she saw all the blood in the bathroom. Aside from that, I don't think it mattered much to her, either way. So afterwards, I got to thinking. Why kill yourself if no one's gonna cry. A stupid reason, right? But any reason's okay."

I didn't know what to say. "I had no idea. I mean, *I'm sorry.*"

She shrugged. "Yeah, I was, too. But don't you see, John, now I'm *glad* it didn't work. Okay, life stinks sometimes, but it's all we've got. Everyone's gotta find something and hang onto it."

I could hardly believe it. Beth Ann had tried to kill herself! What a crappy home life she must have. What a scared, lonely kid she must be. But what was she trying to hang onto at the moment . . . *me?* Yeah, I guess so.

And trying to explain her sudden transformation, too. Had *I* been responsible for that? Sure, I suppose our little talks every day had helped.

"Are you okay?" I asked. "I mean, is everything all right now?"

"Oh, I'm fine; really. That's why I'm telling you all this, understand?"

"Sure I do."

"*Caring* about someone, that's what's important," she continued. "Something like this can happen to *anyone;* even kids with *nice* parents. And we shouldn't feel guilty, don't you agree?"

"Sure I do," I said, trying to reassure her. "Hell, we all have problems."

"That's right, John. So maybe you'd like to sit in on our group sessions sometime. I think you'll find it interesting."

"Me?" I asked, more than a little surprised. But flattered, too. Beth Ann had often expressed interest in my writing; probably she thought this would be a good research experience for me.

It would be quite a responsibility, though: \chronicling\ the psychological problems of American youth. Still, a great writer should be prepared to take on the social conscience of his own generation and deal with the problems that drive kids to despair. Yeah, a subject this big might be even more meaningful than my characterization of Clifford. The second part of my trilogy, maybe.

"There's an adult counselor at each meeting," Beth

Ann explained. "Kids talk about whatever's on their mind. It helps a lot, believe me. I'm going tomorrow night, if you'd like to come."

"Sure, if you don't think I'd be an outsider."

"No one's an outsider, John. That's the whole point."

"And this is a bona fide counseling session, where kids can spill whatever's bothering them?"

"Sure, we're allowed to say anything."

The potential writing material at those sessions would be invaluable. Should I bring my tape recorder or just a notebook? I wondered.

"It's awfully nice of you to do this for me, Beth Ann. Under the circumstances."

"I have to, John," she said, "under the circumstances."

"Okay, I'd like to come."

She smiled. "So writing's still important to you? You're not giving up?"

"*Giving up,* of course not. Where'd you get a crazy idea like that?"

She shook her head. "I don't know, John. Guess I'm not smart enough to figure you out."

I walked Beth Ann home, then kissed her goodnight. Merely a charitable gesture, I thought, made in grateful appreciation. I was surprised at how pleasant it was, so I did it again. I had to bend over, and she had to stand on tiptoe, but it was worth the effort.

"I really like you, John," she whispered. "A lot."

"And I—"

"No, don't say it. In a funny way, it doesn't matter if you care or not, because *I* do. Last year at this time, I didn't care much about anything."

"See you tomorrow night," I said.

"At eight."

She hugged me, then hurried into the lobby.

I walked home feeling great.

A whole new area of research awaited me.

And I felt pleased with myself, too. After all, since knowing me, Beth Ann had turned into a new person: a very sweet, awfully cute one!

Chapter 10

_____

. . . A writer should know too much. . . . E.H.

The next day, I was still the Invisible Man in Holloway's class. That suited me fine, since I had no intention of handing in that sappy essay, after all. New, unplowed fields of literary research awaited me, and I couldn't be bogged down in the mire of Holloway's pedestrian assignments.

Besides, Hollowhead's opinion of my work had suddenly become meaningless. I had more important affirmation of my talents. Beth Ann had shared her true feelings with me. Somehow, she must have sensed that a gifted writer, like a psychiatrist, can look into the human soul and analyze its troubles. I wouldn't disappoint her.

With my confidence returned, I eagerly awaited the new concepts to be explored. I'd soon create a varied patchwork character study of young people set adrift in the city, easy targets for disillusionment. I'd depict their troubles passionately, yet objectively. This was certainly an idea worthy of Book Number Two in my trilogy. I could hardly wait to sit in on my first counseling session and start taking notes.

But where would I find time to return to writing again? At the moment, every spare hour was taken up with butchery. True, I'd grown more used to it, but I still couldn't face the deadly freezer room. (Recently, I'd noticed Mom never went in there, either. Guess only Dad could stomach such savagery.)

Anyway, I'd have to quit. Soon, I'd be visiting Clifford for further research, in addition to beginning my new project. Before long, convicts and suicidal teens would absorb all my time. Working on *two* books at once would be the ultimate challenge of my talent. But first, I'd have to remove myself from the butcher shop.

I decided to bring up the subject that afternoon at work. It was a slow day for customers, so Mom spent most of her time rearranging the salamis into symmetrical patterns.

"Where's Dad? I need to talk to him."

"In the freezer room. He's got special orders to cut. He'll be in there awhile."

Damn. The store was empty, and I didn't want to miss my perfect opportunity to talk with him. If I saved my news until dinnertime, we'd all get indigestion. Dad was sure to give me a hard time about quitting and I wanted to clear the air as quickly as possible.

"Can't he come out for a minute?"

Mom stared at me with a shocked expression, as if I'd asked her to rob a grave or something. "He never comes out until he's finished . . . never."

"How long will that be?"

"Hours. Your father always handles the special cuts himself. And he insists on privacy when he does it. He doesn't even like *me* coming in."

"Well, I have to talk to him; it won't take long."

"He won't like it," she warned, curling the sausages up into S-shaped links in the case.

I decided to risk it. I threw on my sweater and pushed open the door.

"Hi, Dad," I shouted, but he didn't hear me. He was standing by the cutting table in the corner, wearing his pile-lined Levi jacket over his bloodstained butcher apron. I noticed him weaving back and forth in a strange motion, with a peculiar expression on his face; he seemed to be in a daze. Suddenly, he lifted his meat cleaver high in the air while tapping the heel of his foot. Then, swaying side to side, he swung the cleaver down with a vengeance, chopping away at a loin of pork with a furious rhythmic pattern.

What was this . . . Dad's own version of Gestalt therapy? Or was he drunk . . . a closet alcoholic who slipped into the freezer room to take a nip? Maybe that's why Mom wasn't allowed in. No. Dad never consumed more than one glass of beer at a time.

Moving closer, I noticed the tiny earphones he was wearing.

"Hi, Dad," I shouted again, but he still didn't hear me. He smashed the cleaver down again . . . and again . . . continuing the rhythm until he'd transformed the slab of pork into a dozen perfectly severed chops. His eyes sparkled with excitement as he slashed through the remaining gristle with a surgeon's skill. Joszef Sandor, the demon Butcher of Broadway . . . I tell you, he looked weird.

Whatever the sound was that was coming through those earphones, he was totally absorbed. I finally caught his eye, and he switched off the tape recorder in his jacket pocket. Damned if it wasn't a Walkman!

"What are you doing in here, Janos?" he asked (real guiltily, as if I *had* caught him taking a nip). "I'm very busy."

"Sorry, I have to ask you something. Say, I didn't know you had one of those fancy machines."

He grew defensive. "I bought it a while ago. I used to keep a transistor radio back here for music. But all the stations play junk nowadays, nothing good."

"I didn't know you liked music. You never play it at home."

He shrugged. "At home I don't need it. In here, I do."

"What are you listening to?"

He seemed reluctant to answer. "Sarasate's Zigeuner-weisen."

"Huh?"

"Played by Jascha Heifetz."

"Oh. *Classical* stuff."

"Yeah, so?"

"So nothing, I guess."

"So it's no big deal; just a little gypsy melody."

I couldn't understand Dad's reaction. You'd think I'd discovered him in the freezer room with a naked woman or something! Fascinating.

As Dad began wrapping the chops in butcher paper, I sneaked a look at the labels of some other tapes he had stacked above the cutting table. There were selections by Bach, Chausson, Saint-Saëns and others: all violin concertos. Next to the titles, Dad had written special notations: Telemann—flank steak, Bach—venison, Mendelssohn—veal with pockets, etc. Apparently, he had a special musical accompaniment for every piece of meat he cut.

So this was Dad's deep, dark secret. Classical music inspired his butchery! One rhythm was selected for deboning chicken breast, another for cutting up stew. Bet he probably had to play the Anvil Chorus to hack his way through a cow carcass!

I guess Dad figured I'd think it was silly. Actually, I thought it was damn clever. A guy would have to do something to divert himself from the bloody task at hand. But I never thought Dad required such diversion, which made me wonder if he was really the dedicated butcher

I'd always assumed. As he threw a slab of spareribs on the table, I decided to pursue the point.

"So you like music, eh? Ever play an instrument yourself when you were a kid?"

"Never," he said, spreading out the ribs. "But my Uncle Zoltan played the violin. His specialty was Hungarian Rhapsody Number Two. It didn't matter what he played though, he always made the violin cry. And he always promised to teach me when I got older. It never happened. We came to the States and he stayed behind."

"Too bad."

Dad nodded. "Uncle Zoltan has been dead a long time, but I can still hear the beautiful sounds he made."

"So you never got to take lessons."

He smiled philosophically. "Lessons? Things like that were a luxury, son. We were lucky to get out of Hungary with suitcases. Your mother's folks had even less when they arrived. The only thing my father had was a knowledge of the butcher business, so that's what he gave me. Back in the old country, it was expected a son should follow in his father's footsteps. And your Grandpa Bela was a single-minded man. He had to be, to survive the Revolution."

Both my sets of grandparents had died several years before. Maybe people in the old country married late or had real hard lives, because they always looked like they were ancient. Still, I remember Grandpa Bela's look of pride when Dad brought him into the butcher shop for the first time. At least he lived long enough to see that.

I guess it must've been hard for them all, making lives in a new country, with no money or friends. Hard for Mom and Dad, too, though I'd never thought much about it. All those stories about the uprising sounded like B-movie stuff to me when I was little. But now I could see it was probably Dad's sense of duty and tradition that made him so dedicated.

Those old Hungarians were crazy for tradition, especially my Grandpa Bela. Despite a lack of money, he was supposedly descended from royalty. In another century, he might have been a prince or something. And under other circumstances, Dad might have been another Jascha Heifetz, instead of a Paganini of the pork chops, composing adagios for hamhocks and beef bones.

Anyway, my discovery of Dad's secret stash of classical music made me feel more connected to him. Surely, it exhibited an inherent hunger to feed the soul, some untapped creative spirit.

Hell, who knew? Even gifted writers haven't been able to figure out their parents. (Hemingway had a lousy time with his.)

It may have seemed a sappy question, but it was one I'd never asked.

"You do *like* being a butcher, don't you, Dad?"

"I make the best of it. It's decent, hard work. Come rain or shine, people always eat. Is that what you wanted to ask me?"

"No, I just wondered."

"Look, son, when I was a boy in Hungary, I dreamed

of someday going to Budapest to sail down the Danube River. That, I never did. I also dreamed of marrying a beautiful girl who would love me. That, I did do. But I never dreamed of growing up to be a butcher. Does that answer your question?"

"Yeah, I guess so."

"Good. Now let me get back to work, okay?"

"But that's what I came to talk to you about, Dad . . . work."

"Don't worry, Janos, you're doing okay. Already, people have stopped complaining. In a few more months, you'll be all right."

Months? I resented spending another *day* in the shop.

"I won't fire you," he said reassuringly, "if that's what you're worried about. Sometimes customers let off steam, but they always come back."

"No, Dad, that's not it. You see, Beth Ann and I have gotten to know each other lately and . . ."

"Oh, I see," he smiled. "You want a raise . . . some extra cash so you can take her out."

"No, I want some extra *time* . . . so I can work. I want to start writing again."

"I thought you'd given that up."

"Not for good. It's what I want to do . . . with my life, I mean. I don't want to spend it . . ."

"In a butcher shop?"

"Look, maybe *you* don't think I've got talent, but . . ."

"I never said that, son."

"Yeah, well it's obvious, isn't it? But there are more things in life than food, Dad. There's food for the *soul,* too!"

Dad glanced at me with a wistful, faraway expression. "You don't have to tell me that, Janos. I learned it from Uncle Zoltan years ago."

I think I hurt his feelings. "Well, you know what you said about your uncle making the violin cry? I want to do that with *words.*"

"A big ambition."

"You bet. That's why I can't afford to waste time. Beth Ann's given me a whole new idea for a book and I want to work on it.

Dad was silent a moment, then he took a sharp blade from its hook on the wall and sectioned off the spareribs.

"So do it," he said, finally.

"But I'll need time for research."

"So take it."

"Time away from . . . here."

"I understand English, Janos."

"Then I don't have to work here anymore?"

"No, son, you don't *have* to. Your mother thought it might be good for you. But maybe other things are good for you, too; things we don't always understand. That's all right. It's why we came to this country, isn't it? So our children could have freedom of choice. Your grandfather always said that, until the day he died. Write your stories if you want, Janos. After all, me and your mother don't know everything. Maybe you do have talent . . . hidden somewhere we don't know about. Besides, freedom means being able to make mistakes too, right?"

At last. I'd been reprieved! So why did I feel so guilty?

"Thanks, Dad. Guess I'm just not cut out for the butcher business."

"I never said you were. Being a writer is one thing, but being a butcher is something else. I have a talent for it. But you, son, you could live to be a hundred and never learn to put a pocket in a pork chop. That reminds me, I've a special order that needs to be delivered. A new customer, very classy. She called this morning, and I promised it'd be there by five."

"I'll take it over. What is it?"

"Wait'll you see," he said proudly, unwrapping the butcher paper as if it concealed rare rubies.

"Oh," I said, "a ham."

Dad shook his head in disgust. "Janos, to call meat like this ham, is . . . well, it's a sin. This is the finest quality Virginia ham, baked in fruit sauce, then sliced razor thin and tied. One of my specialties. Each slice pulls away like tissue paper. That's what gives it that delicate taste. And the fruit sauce soaks in during baking to keep it moist. This lady said she was having a cocktail party and wanted turkey, can you imagine? I told her this was better."

"Real nice, Dad. Where do I take it?"

"Alicia Fenton, The Schuyler Arms. Here's the apartment number."

"The Schuyler Arms? Is that place finished already?"

"Guess so," he said, scattering fresh parsley on top of the meat, then sealing the package. "Hope it means lots more customers."

I tucked the package under my arm, then headed for the door.

Dad shook his head and sighed. "Janos, I really hope you can be a writer because you'd make a lousy butcher. That isn't dirty laundry you're carrying," he explained, handing me a shopping bag. "It's baked Virginia ham, sliced—"

"Very thin and tied. I know, Dad. And I bet it tastes delicious."

Chapter 11

— — — — — — — — — — —

. . . I have turned down all sorts of propositions and kept the product pure. . . . E.H.

The Schuyler Arms was only a few blocks away and I was anxious to see how it looked, after its renovation. Like the entire West Side, the building had a colorful, varied history. Long ago, when it was built, it must've been quite a place. Since I'd lived in the neighborhood, all that remained to suggest its former elegance was the architecture: ornate balconies, circular windows and a fancy domed entrance secluded from the street.

Like many buildings, it had fallen on hard times and become an SRO. For years, every crook, transvestite, hooker, addict and pimp retreated behind its walls when things got hot. Drug deals, murders, *everything* went on in there. Sometimes, its vice and corruption spilled out onto the street in the form of burning mattresses and smashed booze bottles. Anyone with sense knew enough to steer clear of the sidewalk, when passing by.

So it went, until a year ago. An enterprising businessman bought the building, evicted all the scuzz, then remodeled it as a co-op. Now, it supposedly boasted Old World elegance, penthouse gardens and duplex apartments.

The change was definitely dramatic. The entrance court had been refinished in terra-cotta tiles, with potted plants and flowers encircling the corners. There was a glass elevator in the entrance lobby and a liveried doorman at the desk.

"I have a package for Fenton."

He looked at me disdainfully, then picked up the intercom. "There's a person here with a package," he announced, with nauseating superiority. "Miss Fenton wants to know if you're the butcher."

"Yeah, I'm the butcher," I said, dumping the bag on the desk. "Should I leave it here?"

Apparently, he found the thought appalling. "Apartment Seven E, through the atrium."

An atrium, yet. I felt like telling the guy I knew the place when . . . when you couldn't come inside without getting your throat slit! Were the new tenants as snooty as the help?

I walked through the glass-enclosed courtyard, rode

the glass elevator and rang the bell. When the door opened, I didn't care if the girl who answered it was snooty or not. She was gorgeous. About eighteen, I guessed, but hard to tell. She had a maturity that only comes from the self-assurance of wealth, ritzy finishing schools, summers in Monte Carlo and winters on the Austrian slopes. Classy, down to her fingertips. Tall, with long blonde hair. Maybe it came from a bottle, but an expensive one. She wore a red silk thing, like pajamas, but probably the latest, chic-est, in-est fashion from Paris or wherever.

"Ah, the butcher," she said, "with manna from heaven."

"It's a ham," I answered stupidly.

"A delicious one, I hope. You saved my life, Mr. Sandor. Dad's having a zillion guests descend in moments, and all I could think of when I called you this morning was turkey, imagine. Of course, our housekeeper usually does the ordering, but she's still on Long Island, packing things. While here we are, with practically nothing."

She gestured around the living room. The "nothing" consisted of a long suede sofa, a white fur carpet and lots of brass tables.

"It's a housewarming," she explained. "Apartment-warming, actually. But nothing's been done, and *every-one's* coming."

"Yeah, well here's the meat."

"I can barely wait to taste it. The way you described it, it must be ambrosia."

It seemed pointless to mention that I wasn't the person she'd spoken with on the phone. She was confused enough already.

There was a loud bang from somewhere downstairs, and a voice shouted, "Ali, I think Igor got into the canapes!"

With noisy thuds, a giant Russian wolfhound came bounding up the stairs of the duplex with a tablecloth in his teeth.

"You wretched boy," she shouted, chasing him around the room until she'd retrieved the cloth. "He's simply mad about Brie."

"Where should I put the meat?"

"Be an angel and take it to the kitchen? Igor has *cheese* all over his paws."

"Which way?"

"First door on the left, down the stairs."

My purple joggers squeaked along the polished parqueted floors. Damn, the place was big: room after room filled with unopened crates, lots of them stamped from foreign countries. Whoever this Fenton guy was, he must travel a lot.

The kitchen was a typical *House Beautiful* number, with butcher blocks, a microwave and built-in everything. I checked the corners for empty bottles of Ripple, left by previous tenants. Instead, I found cases of Dom Perignon champagne stacked by the fridge. And the table was loaded with fancy nibbles: caviar and peacock tongues, probably. But all the smelly cheeses were on the floor, obviously where Igor left them. I figured the empty silver platter was meant for the meat, so I stuck the ham on it. Since Dad's reputation hung in the balance, I rearranged the parsley.

When I was ready to leave, a large, burly man pushed through the door, struggling with his necktie. "Ali, I refuse to wear this thing. Why must you always dress me like a monkey?" He glanced around. "Where's my daughter?"

"Upstairs with the dog."

"Good," he said, ripping the necktie off and sticking it in the cabinet. He was a bear of a man, with a long gray beard and a barrel chest. And he looked familiar. "Don't tell her where the damn thing is, okay? It's bad enough I have to wear *shoes* at this shindig."

"You aren't," I said, noticing his feet.

He looked down with annoyance. "You're right. Hell, I don't suppose sneakers'd do—or sandals, maybe."

Miss Fenton appeared in the doorway, surveying her father coolly. "Father, you're not dressed. Where's your necktie?"

"Igor ate it," he said, quite seriously.

Then she noticed his feet. *"Father.* Gucci delivered a lovely pair of loafers earlier; I ordered them especially. They're in your room."

"Damn it, Ali, do I have to?"

"Of course. Your guests will be here any minute."

"Your guests, you mean. Don't see why *I* have to be uncomfortable. Hell, I've entertained the Dalai Lama,

maharajahs, and the King of Tonga; and not one of them looked at my feet!"

"You're not in the *jungle,* now, Father."

The poor guy looked like a trapped animal trying to escape his deadly fate. As a final protest, he gestured to me.

"What about him? He's not wearing fancy duds."

"Father, that's the *butcher.*"

"It is? Well good, have him stay. *I* need someone to talk to at this party, too." He headed for the door. "And if I hear too much literary crap, Igor and I will lock ourselves in the john."

Alicia Fenton flashed me an embarrassed smile. "You must excuse my father. He's been at sea for over a year. Literally that is, not metaphorically."

From her aloof tone, I'd bet a million she thought I didn't know what metaphorical meant. In spite of her fantastic looks, I decided not to like her. A little la-de-da in a girl is okay, but she carried it too far. And I couldn't match her up with the regular guy who was supposed to be her father.

"At sea? Is he in the navy?"

"No, doing research for a book," she explained, rearranging the hors d'oeuvres. "He sailed his schooner around the Cape of Good Hope. For a while, we thought he sank in the Indian Ocean. But Father's indomitable. He once lived with Micronesian cannibals and lived to tell the tale."

Fenton: the name suddenly clicked. *Alexander Fen-*

ton: the most famous adventure writer of the century. I'd gobbled up his books when I was younger. Fenton had been everywhere and done everything. As a reporter, he was in the thick of it during the Vietnam War, writing his articles as bombs exploded around him. He'd climbed to the top of Mount Everest, been sponge diving in the Mediterranean, worked on an oil-rig at sea and headed a search party through Tibet, tracking down the Yeti. Each of his adventures he turned into an exciting tale of action and intrigue.

I couldn't believe it. I was standing in Alexander Fenton's kitchen! No wonder he looked familiar. I'd seen his face on book jackets a dozen times. Fenton: the man's man, who'd challenged nature and the elements and won. Ironic, to see him cowering in his own kitchen, fighting over wearing shoes.

"I'm afraid Father's a little rough around the edges at present. He's always like this when he returns from a trip. He simply loses all social graces. Naturally, I don't expect you to stay."

Miss Fenton was too la-de-da to tell me to buzz off. And I was too damn interested to leave. A party hosted by Fenton would probably draw every literary name in town.

"But I'd like to stay."

She backed away as if I'd slapped her, then regained her cool. "Then you must, of course. After all, you were invited."

I toyed with the idea of confessing I wasn't a butcher

at all, but a talented, aspiring writer with literary credentials of my own. I didn't. Let her think she was entertaining a Neanderthal; it served her right.

"I do wish Serena were here," she pouted. "I've misplaced the glasses."

I checked the cupboard. "Here they are."

She began taking them down. "Our guests will be here any moment, and nothing's ready. I suppose I should have waited to give this party, but if I had, Father wouldn't have allowed it. He's a bear about such things. I have to surprise him with social functions, or he doesn't show up at all. Imagine, he didn't think we needed this pied-à-terre. He's perfectly happy poking along the beach with Igor. Of course, out of season, East Hampton's a dreadful bore."

She was about to add, "don't you think?" but thought better of it.

Despite her superior attitude, I felt a little sorry for La Fenton. She'd probably never set foot in a kitchen before and was helpless without help.

"Want me to clean up the mess on the floor and bring up the champagne?"

"Would you? You're an angel. There's tons of it chilling in the fridge."

Relieved of her cumbersome burden, she wafted up the stairs just as the bell rang.

I still couldn't believe I was in the home of Alexander Fenton. What writing expertise he must have locked in his head, what guidance and advice. What a coup, to be in the presence of a literary *master*. He rarely appeared in public, never gave interviews, didn't even like to have his picture taken for book jackets.

Hurriedly, I cleared up the cheesy mess, then put some bottles of champagne on a tray. I could hear the place filling upstairs with laughter, "darlings" and "how are you's." What other literary giants were walking above my head? Balancing the tray, I went to see.

The place was crammed all right, but I couldn't spy Fenton. And I didn't know why his daughter worried about his outfit. Lots of her guests looked like deadbeats, in old jeans and sneakers. Maybe they were literary deadbeats, which makes a difference. Others were dressed to the teeth, though: silk-this and cashmere-that.

I made my way through the crowd, trying not to spill champagne on a shoe, bag or jacket some poor cow had given her life for.

Alicia Fenton wasn't just minus a housekeeper; she didn't have chairs, either. But the oversight pleased everyone. Her well-dressed guests realized standing at cocktail parties is de rigueur. The seedy types couldn't wait to schlump on the floor.

I put the tray on the table before people started thinking I was hired help.

"We've tons of food in the kitchen," Miss Fenton announced, "if only some able-bodied souls would bring it up."

"Ali, a do-it-yourself-party? How inspired!"

Like a shot, guests were rushing up and down the

stairs: carrying trays, pouring champagne and passing hors d'oeuvres. Dad's ham was soon being devoured like Christians by the lions!

Alicia Fenton looked relieved; her lack of organization had been misinterpreted for originality. Now, her only remaining problem was *me*. Nervously, she glanced over several times, hoping I wasn't picking my nose or something equally offensive. I considered it, but was more interested in making contact with recognizable authors or publishers. Maybe I'd get someone's ear and mention my blockbuster book. So what if it was only fifty-two pages? I'd heard that million dollar advances were offered for less: a chapter, even an outline.

Elbowing my way through the elbow-patch set, I began picking up threads of conversation. . . .

"A fresh look at the Peloponnesian War? Long overdue, but you've got to get a grant."

"There's no such thing as writer's block. When I have to grind it out, I grind it out."

"Dried up, my dear. His last book was maddening in its vagueness."

"So I told him. No one knows more about disassociation than I do. . . ."

I couldn't get a word in anywhere! A woman with a mountain of hair and tons of ethnic jewelry shoved a glass of champagne at me. I slugged it down, continuing to ferret out a hole in someone's conversation.

I found something better. Alexander Fenton was seated on the floor in the corner. The plant in front of him and the huge dog on his lap all but obscured him from view. If it hadn't been for his *grass sandals* poking out, *I* might've missed him, too.

I caught his eye and he gestured me over. As I squeezed down beside him, he rearranged the hulky canine.

"Make room for a working man, Igor."

The dog whined and rolled over.

"Smelly cheeses," Fenton explained, "they're his weakness. Too rich for his blood, but he doesn't care." He glanced at his daughter, who was laughing across the room. "We all have weaknesses. Ali's mine. Never refuse her anything . . . finishing schools that finished her and parties that make my teeth ache. Funny thing is, *I* don't have to be here. Once the babble starts, it gains momentum, feeding off itself. Cellular conversational crap. You know, there's a tribe in Bora Bora with an interesting penal system. When a tribesman is found guilty of murder, he's placed in a field and everyone keeps talking at him until he's dead."

"Is that true?"

Fenton smiled, wrinkling up tanned layers of skin. "No, but I bet it would work."

The look he threw me seemed like a life raft he was trying to grab onto. I got the impression he felt I was the only *regular* person in the room, besides himself.

"What's your name?" he asked.

"John Sandor."

He shook my hand. I couldn't believe it. I was seated

at the feet of Alexander Fenton, who'd just shaken my hand with a strong, decisive, determined grip.

"I'm surprised you're still here, Sandor. I figured all this talk would send you running back to your butcher shop, like the sensible person you seem to be."

"I'm not really a butcher," I confessed.

His expression grew guarded. "What are you then?"

I wanted to reveal that *I* was a writer, too: a struggling, totally dedicated one. But instinct warned me that that would send Fenton running for the hills.

"I'm a student."

He chuckled and scratched Igor's neck. "Wonder why Ali thinks you're a butcher. Hell, it doesn't matter. She thinks everyone here's a *writer*."

"Aren't they?"

He laughed out loud. "This bunch? Not one in the lorryload, son. Know what Carl Sandburg called them? The Abracadabra Boys! He had their number. But poor Ali doesn't know the difference."

Apparently, neither did I.

"Well, they're all talking about writing," I said.

He nodded. *"That's* the difference, buddy-boy. The *real* writers are light years from here . . . slaving over typewriters, starving, retching, smoking their guts out, feeling utterly miserable and inadequate . . . convinced every word they put down is garbage. This crowd's all imposters: laughing, well-fed phonies. But Ali, in the full-blown innocence of youth, can't see that. She prefers the romanticized cocktail party image, ignoring the reality.

Namely, that true writers are surly, driven, antisocial and obsessed . . . like me."

I knew enough about obsession to realize that what Fenton said might be true. But his image of the dedicated writer seemed slanted. After all, he'd seen the world, had fame and glory, made a fortune. He must have dropped a bundle on this duplex, in which he was presently hiding in the corner .

"Maybe *your* image of writers is romanticized, too." I suggested.

Fenton stared at me, as if reevaluating our conversation.

"You lied to me, boy. I'd hoped you were a butcher, but you're a student. Now it turns out you're a *clever* one. And a perspiring writer, too, I'll bet. It's written all over that earnest face. You're a disappointment, son."

Fenton tried looking serious. But I sensed, if not saw, a wink in his eye. I think he liked me.

"Mr. Fenton, why don't you teach and lecture; share your knowledge?"

"Haven't any," he said, taking a flask from his back pocket. "Share my booze with you, though."

Under the circumstances, I couldn't refuse, so I took a slug. A vile liquid slid down my throat, instantly setting fire to my stomach.

"What *is* that?" I asked, after lots of coughing.

"Rotgut." He laughed, slapping me on the back. "Now isn't it time you told me about your book?"

I stared blankly.

"You've got one, haven't you? An original some-thing-or-other. A breakthrough concept that'll revolu-tionize the writing field?"

The man was really brilliant! "Yeah, how did you know?"

"A lucky guess. What's it about?"

He offered me his flask again, and I didn't refuse. My head swimming with excitement and liquor, I de-scribed my work-in-progress. I tried not to omit the most relevant details. I explained it was a book of epic propor-tions, told through the eyes of a flower-loving ex-con; the first in a trilogy depicting urban inhumanity.

Fenton didn't interrupt me once. In fact, he listened with more than passing interest. As people pushed by, glasses clinked, conversations grew louder, Fenton con-tinued to listen.

In those moments of elation, I envisioned him soon pounding on the door of his publisher's office, insisting my masterpiece be read immediately. Suddenly, all the suf-fering I'd endured seemed worthwhile. Fenton had finally discovered a precocious protégé worthy of him: someone to open his mind to . . . take for cruises on the old Windjammer or whatever . . . a talented newcomer to share all his knowledge.

"Well, that's it," I concluded. "Of course, I've hardly begun the book, but that's the general idea."

He was silent a moment, obviously absorbing the magnitude of my work. Then he asked, "Know much about flowers?"

"No, nothing. But—"

"Ever been in prison?"

"Of course not. But my friend, Clifford, has."

Fenton nodded, then scratched Igor's stomach.

"Son, I'll give you some good advice, which you won't have to pay to hear at a lecture, which I refuse to give, anyway."

"Yes?"

"Books are like muffins. You should always throw the first batch out!"

Taking another slug from his flask, he stood up to leave. I stifled an impulse to grab him by the legs! I couldn't let him go. I must have described the book badly. Something of such epic dimensions had to be *read,* not talked about. Writers are notoriously poor at describing their own stuff, anyway; everyone knows that.

"I could *show* you the book," I said. "I only live a few blocks away."

Fenton didn't hear me. The minute he stood up, he became a target for everyone in the room.

"Alex, where have you been *hiding?*"

"Alex, the place is fantastic. Have you picked a room to work in yet?"

"Love those sandals, Alex. They're divine."

"Who's this young man who's been monopolizing you all evening?"

He smiled. "A writer, naturally. Aren't we all? Excuse me, I think Igor's gonna be sick."

Grabbing the dog by the collar, he made a hasty

retreat. I tried following, but got sucked up in the crunch. After a moment, all I could see was Igor's tail, bouncing down the stairs.

"Known Alex long?" a voice asked.

I nodded no, too upset to talk.

Someone passed by with a tray of drinks and I took one; then another.

Throw my book out; that had been Fenton's advice. Ridiculous. The old guy must be suffering from seasickness or jungle rot. No wonder he didn't lecture. Who'd listen to crappy advice like that?

Maybe he was prejudiced, harboring a secret hatred for ex-cons, or jealous of new blood, pushing him from the limelight. Sure, that was it. He'd already downgraded every other writer in the room; now it was my turn.

I solaced myself with more champagne and a desperate attempt to lose myself in conversation. Two tweedy types were arguing about the Russian Revolution, something I knew zip about, but I decided to join in.

"The Bolsheviks screwed up," one guy said. "They never should've gotten rid of the Czar."

"That's half-assed thinking, George."

"It sure is," I agreed. (I could feel myself bobbing and weaving, grateful the room was so crowded; I had no space to fall down.) "What they shouldn't have done is teach people to *read*. Societies always screw up when people learn to read."

The gray-haired guy named George patted me on

the back, as if I'd said something brilliant. Maybe I had. To celebrate the fact, I grabbed another glass of champagne.

"That's radical thinking, fella," the other guy argued. "You a Royalist or what?"

All I knew for certain was I'd gotten the royal brush-off from Fenton and was now getting drunk as a skunk!

"A Royalist?" I muttered. "Yeah, maybe so. My dad says his family goes all the way back to Transylvanian princes."

"Is that so?"

"Damn right. And all revolutions stink. He remembers the Hungarian one and it smelled. He might have been a Heifetz, but now all he has is earphones. It's very sad."

To my horror, I felt a tear forming in my left eye. Hell, was I turning into one of those crying drunks who slobber over everyone?

"Your father fought in the Hungarian Revolution?"

The room was getting larger, then smaller, and I didn't know why.

"No, *his* father, Bela Sandor. He was a butcher, too. From a long line of 'em, until I broke the link. One missing sausage link and all those butchers fall down, isn't that awful?"

Damn, the place was hot! As the walls kept closing in, words kept pouring out. And the two guys (now practically holding me up) seemed awfully interested.

147

"*Bela,* you're kidding; that's really a name? He fought in the Hungarian Revolution?"

"Sure, my mom's folks did, too. Both of them came here as kids. Just some ratty suitcases and stories about the Evil Eye. No uncles. No violins . . . nothing." My stomach rolled over "Are you guys hot or what?"

They glanced at each other, then dragged me toward a window.

"Here, get some air," said George, easing me down to the floor.

"This is good material," said the other guy, "never used."

I thought they were talking about my clothes. "Na, they're second hand. Murphy's a real good egg."

"Was he in the Resistance army, too?"

"No, the *Salvation* Army." I laughed, which made my head pound like a rock band was rehearsing inside.

About then, I realized I'd lost the thrust of the conversation. Oh, I was still talking, but I wasn't sure of what I was saying, or why. I think it had something to do with butchers, the Carpathian Mountains and the eternal struggle for freedom of expression. Hell, I don't know. All I knew for certain is that these two guys were interested. In fact, one took out a pad and began taking notes. As I kept rambling on, they nodded their heads like goofy wooden dolls. The rhythm was making me nauseated.

Eventually, someone breezed by with a tray of coffee cups, and George had sense enough to hand me one. That and the fresh air coming through the window helped. The walls began receding, and the ceiling spun more slowly. I began to see faces again. Across the room, Alicia Fenton was staring at me as if I had two heads. The joke was on her: she was the one with all the extra eyeballs!

I glanced over and noticed that George had scribbled his way through half a pad of paper.

"This is all very interesting," he said excitedly. "What's your name?"

"John Sandor." (Probably, the first *sensible* thing I'd said.) "What's yours?"

"George Ramsey. And this is my partner, Alfred Leland. We've collaborated on lots of books: *factual,* historical stuff. Ever read *Where Hath Freedom Gone?*"

"Never."

"It's our latest. We take history and see it through the eyes of real people, ordinary ones. This Grandpa Bela business is perfect for us, right Alfred?"

Alfred nodded. "Tailor made."

"There's built-in symbolism here, John. The butchery of society, seen through the eyes of a real butcher. Simple, raw clarity, made to grab the reader. Our first step would be to interview your father, make a few tapes, right, Alfred?"

Alfred nodded.

"Get down his life experiences in his own words: the horrors of war, readjustment as an immigrant, introduction to democracy—that stuff."

This time, Alfred didn't nod. "I don't know, George. Maybe we're off-base here. After all, that thing in the fifties wasn't a *real* revolution."

"What would you call it then?" George argued. "Hundreds of people were executed; thousands imprisoned."

Alfred reconsidered. "Okay, let's go with it. The human interest'll overpower the details, anyway. Your father speaks English, doesn't he, John? Where's his butcher shop?"

"And what about Grandpa Bela? Is he still alive?"

"My *grandfather?* He's been dead for years. How'd you know about him?"

"You told us, of course. Great background stuff. But he's dead, eh? Well, no problem. We can still use him with a literary flashback."

The black coffee was slowly beginning to sober me up, pulling me back to reality. When I arrived, I didn't like what I saw. Apparently, I'd spilled my entire family history to these jerks, who were now picking over it like vultures.

"There's a statement to be made here, Alfred. We can get in the religious thing, too. That's topical again."

Alfred resumed nodding.

The nerve of these guys! Leeches, vampires; sucking the juices from other people's experience. Filing things away, sifting them in a pot, spitting them out as a book.

Maybe if they *knew* my family, it would be different. But they were pulling apart our lives, diagramming them, without caring who we really were. Hacks, hacking away. Snooping and nosing around, wanting to tape interviews, *all for a lousy book.* If anyone wrote about my family, it should be *me.* After all, I was the one who . . .

. . . I got a sickening feeling in my stomach, and it wasn't the booze. In that instant, I suddenly realized there weren't *two* vultures in the room, but *three.*

I was one, too.

Maybe lots of life's meaningful moments arrive that way; like a hit on the head or a punch in the gut. This one sure did. Suddenly, I saw myself in all my splendor: bothering the Mancussos, confusing poor pitiful Grendel; picking away at Clifford. I wasn't following in the footsteps of literary giants, wasn't breaking new ground. I was a butcher, just like these guys. Cutting up other people's lives. A cannibal, feeding on other people's adventures. Unlike Alexander Fenton: everything *he* wrote came from first-hand experience. He'd lived, endured, survived and recounted it. He wrote what he knew and believed, not what someone else knew and believed.

It's truly crappy sitting on the floor in a roomful of strangers, wanting to throw up and feeling a failure.

Personal experience; that was the key. But I had none. No trips to Bora Bora, no conquests of Everest; I couldn't swim, and I'd probably get seasick on a boat. What was left? Nothing. Oh, maybe I had a talent for stringing words together, but who cared? Writers like that are Alfred and George, roaming cocktail parties, hoping to meet Hungarian butchers. No wonder Fenton despised them. I bet he and Igor were hiding in the john this minute!

"Well, what do you think?" asked Alfred. "We'll change the names, if you like. But we've gotta keep Bela. Anyway, we'll let your folks see the final draft, for sure. No approval though, just a look-see, okay?"

George's and Alfred's sickly white faces pressed down on me. Any minute, their vampire teeth would protrude, clamping onto my jugular, sucking out my Hungarian blood.

I still wasn't totally sober, but I was getting there. "You guys do this for a living or what?"

"Of course," said George. "We're writers."

"No, you're not. If you were, you'd be in a room somewhere, convinced you're garbage."

"What're you talking, garbage? This is a great idea. Your parents lived through a piece of history. We can tap that source material and have a blockbuster book. Guess you don't know much about writing, John; that's how it's done."

Alfred nodded. "Right. This story's got epic proportions."

His pompous words sounded awfully familiar. I thought of my talk with Fenton. Damn, what a bozo he must've thought I was, shoving my book at him, like it was *War and Peace*. In his day, Fenton had dined with pygmies and princes, but until now, he'd probably never met a genuine member of the booboisie!

"Excuse me," I said, getting up. "I think I'm gonna be sick."

My legs felt like rubber bands as I pushed my way through the noisy crowd, with George and Alfred following close behind.

"I've gotta get down your address," George insisted.

"And your phone number," added Alfred.

"Sorry, fellas. If you wanna write about a revolution, start your own!"

Struggling toward the door, I could hear Alicia Fenton's laughter echoing after me.

Maybe she wasn't laughing at me, but she should've been!

Chapter 12

— — — — — — — — — —

. . . good writers always come back. Always. . . . E.H.

I was glad to hit the street and clear the old head. Yeah, that's what it felt like: a tired, old, empty head. It was no small accomplishment to be both a hack and a has-been at the age of sixteen. But where would that experience get me?

Still feeling sorry for myself, I remembered my appointment with Beth Ann at eight. I'd have to cancel. No matter how good the story, I wouldn't be one of those bloodsuckers, like Alfred and George.

I checked the clock in a nearby grocery: ten past eight. Beth Ann would probably be waiting at the butcher shop. I hurried up Broadway and found her standing outside. Dad had already closed up and gone home.

"John, I was worried. Your dad said you should have been back hours ago. What happened?"

"I was making a delivery."

"Where to, *New Jersey?*"

"No, light years from here. Another world."

"Quit fooling; tell me."

"It's true. I've come back from the Twilight Zone. When I left, I was a talented young writer; now I'm a hack."

She stared at me. "Have you been drinking?"

"Yeah, rotgut and champagne. They don't mix."

"Is that *all* you had?"

"Isn't that enough?"

"Well, you're sure talking crazy. We'd better walk fast; we're already late."

I stopped her at the corner. "I'm not going with you, Beth Ann."

"Why not?"

"I can't. I won't be a vulture or leech anymore. I'll stop writing *forever* before I do that."

"Don't say that, John, you've *got* to come. Especially if you feel like that."

"Look, I know what you're trying to do for me, but it won't work. Let's face it; I'm a washout."

"Come on," she said, dragging me into the corner coffee shop. "Let's have a soda."

We sat down in a booth, and she ordered for both of us.

"Listen, I don't wanna hold you up," I said. "Go on without me."

"No way," she insisted. "You need this group more than I do. What happened, anyway? Yesterday, you *wanted* to go."

"Yeah, but that's before I met the enemy and found out he's me."

"Damn it, John," she said impatiently. "Cut the fancy junk. You know I don't understand it."

"That's what I'm trying to do, Beth Ann, cut through the crap. That's why I don't want to sit in a roomful of kids with problems, taking notes."

"Notes? What do you mean?"

"I want to be a *real* writer; not someone who feeds off other people's experiences. Sure, I'll admit I thought it was a great idea to tape record one of your sessions, but—"

"*Tape record?*" she asked, nearly choking on her soda.

"Yeah, I know it's a great story. But it's not for me, not anymore."

If looks could kill, Beth Ann's would have totalled me.

"John Sandor, you're a *jackass!* Is that why you thought I wanted you to come along? Dumb research?"

"Sure, what else?"

"Because you're sick," she shouted. "Messed-up. Trying to *kill yourself*, that's why."

"Me? Whatever gave you a crazy idea like that?"

"*You* did, that night at the monument; talking about burials and stuff."

I still couldn't remember whatever dramatic statement I might've made that night.

"You said it was all over," she reminded me.

"Oh that. I was talking about my book."

"Your *book?* You mean I've been tracking you like a bloodhound for weeks, when all you were upset about was a lousy *book?*"

"Tracking me?"

"Sure. I've been going to your folks' store every day to make sure you're all right. You're worse than a jackass, John. You're an *idiot.* I knocked myself out, trying to make contact. To make you see I cared. It was like pulling teeth, getting you to talk, but I did it. Guess I'm a prize jackass, too. You never even noticed."

I stared blankly as Beth Ann began to cry.

"Lemme get this straight. You mean you asked me to come to the session because you thought *I* was thinking of suicide?"

"Of course I did, you dope. I thought you were ready to check out, just like I was last year. I wanted to *help.*"

I suddenly recalled all Beth Ann's visits to the store; the great conversations we'd had. Hell, I thought she was only flirting.

"But Beth Ann, I thought you did that because you liked me."

"*Of course* I like you, you big . . . oh, never mind. I've gotta go. Listen, John, I'm glad to hear you're not suicidal. But you're still a big mess in my book!"

"Listen, let me walk you."

"Don't bother, stay where you are. I don't think that swelled head of yours will fit through the door, anyway." She threw down some change for the sodas. "Just for the record, did you mean any of those things you said? About my looking good without make-up, being pretty?"

"Sure I did, every word."

"That's something, I guess. I'd hate to think I threw out all those lipsticks for nothing."

"Hey, don't leave like this. Are you okay?"

"Sure, whatever steam I need to let off can go at the session. That's what they're for."

"I'll come, if you like."

"No thanks," she said. "You don't belong. This group is for people with *feelings.* So long, John."

"People with feelings" . . . the words haunted my walk home, while specters floated in front of me. In the darkness behind the streetlights, flimsy images of Beth Ann, Holloway, Fenton and my folks huddled and whispered together. . . .

"I don't understand it. Janci was always such a clever boy."

"Clever's not enough. You must have *feelings,* too."

"Janos, we finally got the medical report. Bad news. You have no *heart.*"

"Sorry buddy, you're just another Abracadabra boy."

"Poor John. Now you have nothing to write about

. . . ever again . . . ever again". . . .

Their smoky shadows faded into nothingness, and in
their place stood a tired old man in gypsy garb playing
his violin. His music was soft and sweet, its strains carrying
joy and bitterness, happiness and sorrow. As he plucked
the nonexistent strings, each note evoked a corresponding
feeling somewhere inside me: an emotion that raced
through my veins with a pulsing rhythm, awakening
feelings I hadn't known existed.

Then suddenly, he was gone, and I found myself
standing alone as if I'd traveled through some uncharted
time frame of the soul, only to arrive at the dead-end of
my own doorstep, empty once again.

I hurried into the building, hoping to put the ghostly
apparitions behind me. As I entered the apartment, I
must have looked like a ghost myself.

"Janci, what's wrong? You look awful."

"Where were you?" asked Dad. "Did you deliver
that ham?"

"The ham? Oh, yeah."

"And they liked it?"

"Sure. They let me stay for the party."

"That nice girl was asking for you, Janci."

"Yeah, I saw her."

"It's getting late. Better do your homework."

"Sure, Dad."

Undaunted, the gypsy specter, who was surely Uncle
Zoltan, had pursued me to my room to continue his bitter-

sweet refrain. Like Jacob Marley arousing the conscience of Scrooge, or Hamlet's father's ghost reminding him of ancestral obligations, he seemed to be suggesting mine should be put right by writing.

Was it possible? Did I have something to write about, after all? Yes, it came to me like a blessing, but a mixed one; mingling pain and confusion.

I took my typewriter from the closet and put it on my desk. As if in a daze, I typed out the title for Mr. Holloway's assignment: My Friend. Somehow, it didn't seem superficial anymore.

Beth Ann was a friend, a *real* one, though I hadn't known it. All the qualities Mom and Dad had seen so easily were only now becoming apparent to me. I began by describing the look on her face that day outside the butcher shop and the contrasting one I'd seen just minutes before she left me. And the funny walk she had, as if always on tiptoe.

Important things, too: her generosity and caring. I needed to tell all about the person I'd found inside.

I felt unequal to the task. After all, I only had a talent for stringing words together. Describing Beth Ann required *heart,* something I'd never tapped before. But I pulled the feelings out as best I could. I dug deeper than I ever had, laying out my emotions on the blank, white paper.

Papa Hemingway's words gave me confidence. He'd said sometimes writing was like drilling rock, then blasting it out with charges.

It took me hours, but when I finished, I knew it was the first *true* thing I'd ever written. Simple and honest. I hoped Holloway would think so, too.

Anyway, Uncle Zoltan must've approved. By the time I finished, his vapory vision had disappeared, taking with it the last soulful strains of melodic music. And I was left with only me for company. I found myself to be not quite so brilliant and self-assured as I'd imagined, but not as hopeless as I'd supposed.

As a final gesture, I began writing a note to Mr. Holloway. In the assignment, I hadn't mentioned Beth Ann by name, not wanting to embarrass her. But now, I didn't mind embarrassing myself. I told him I'd been a prize jackass and I knew it!

By then it was past midnight, but I had to make a phone call. I stumbled through the darkened living room and dialed Beth Ann's number.

"Hi, it's me, John. I know it's late but—"

"That's okay, I'm glad you called. I wanted to say I'm sorry."

"Really? That's what I wanted to say."

"Really? That's nice. Are you all right?"

"Me? Sure. And you?"

"I'm fine. The session helped. But I'm glad you don't need them, John. I didn't mean what I said before. You're not a mess and that's good."

"Oh, but I am, Beth Ann. A big mess. I only realized it tonight."

"Did you? Oh, that's wonderful. I mean . . ."

"I know what you mean. I wanted to say something else. Thank you. Thank you for being my friend."

"Oh, John, you'll make me cry."

"Damn, don't do that. I hate going out with girls who cry."

"Are you asking me for a date or what?"

"I think it's 'or what.' I mean, no it's not a date exactly. How'd you like to take a bus ride with me this weekend? Up to Fishkill, New York."

"Fishkill? What for?"

"I'd like to visit someone. A convict in prison up there. His name's Clifford Karlbach. He loves flowers, and he's a real great guy."

"What's this for, research?"

"No way. Just a visit to a friend. The ride should be nice, what do you say?"

She laughed. "It sounds a little crazy, but okay."

"Good. And Beth Ann, I promise not to bring a tape recorder . . . not even a pad and pencil. From now on, that's not my style!"